THE
CHILDREN'S TREASURY
OF
Fairy Tales

THE
CHILDREN'S TREASURY
OF
Fairy Tales

Ariel Books

**Andrews McMeel
Publishing**

Kansas City

THE CHILDREN'S TREASURY OF FAIRY TALES copyright © 1991, 1992, 1995, 1996, and 2000 by Armand Eisen. All rights reserved. Printed in Singapore. No part of this book may be used or reproduced in any manner whatsoever without written permission except in the case of reprints in the context of reviews. For information write Andrews McMeel Publishing, an Andrews McMeel Universal company, 4520 Main Street, Kansas City, Missouri 64111.

www.andrewsmcmeel.com

Cover painting by Ruth Sanderson

ISBN: 1-58209-048-3

CONTENTS

THE
CHILDREN'S TREASURY
OF
Fairy Tales

THE UGLY DUCKLING

By HANS CHRISTIAN ANDERSEN

Retold by JENNIFER GREENWAY

Illustrated by ROBYN OFFICER

One lovely summer day, on the bank of a quiet pond beside an old farmhouse, a duck sat on her nest waiting for her eggs to hatch.

First a crack appeared on one egg, then on another, and another. Little ducklings began to poke their heads out of the shells.

The mother duck was delighted until she noticed that one egg still had not hatched. This egg was larger than the others and a dull gray color.

The mother duck sighed. She was about to sit on the nest awhile longer when one of the older ducks in the pond came by. She asked the mother duck about her ducklings and then said, "I wouldn't bother trying to hatch that egg if I were you. It looks like a turkey egg to me. I hatched one once by mistake, and it

caused me no end of trouble. Leave that egg alone and come teach your ducklings to swim!"

But the mother duck replied that she had been sitting on her nest so long already, a little more time wouldn't matter. And she settled onto her nest and waited patiently.

Presently, the mother duck heard a sharp crack, and out popped the last duckling. But what a strange duckling he was! He was twice as big as the others, and had gray feathers instead of yellow.

Even his mother had to admit he was rather ugly. "Oh, dear," she thought. "Perhaps it was a turkey egg after all!"

The next morning, she led her ducklings to the pond to teach them how to swim. The ugly duckling jumped right in the water and swam with no trouble.

"Well, he can't be a turkey, if he can swim as well as that," his mother said to herself. "Besides, if you look at him properly, he isn't so ugly!"

Feeling very proud, the mother duck called her ducklings out of the water. Then she led them to the barnyard to introduce them to the other ducks.

"Be sure to behave yourselves," she told them as they walked through the grass. "And don't forget to say 'quack' and bow politely to everyone."

In the barnyard, the ducklings did as they were told. They bowed politely to everyone and said "quack." The other ducks looked them over carefully. "Your ducklings are all very well behaved," one of the old ducks said at last. "And they are all very pretty—except for that big gray one. He is the ugliest duckling I've ever seen!"

All the other ducks in the barnyard agreed, and even the ugly duckling's brothers and sisters began to make fun of him.

"He is ugly," replied his mother, "but he is clever and polite and means no harm."

"Very well," sniffed the other ducks. "He can stay, so long as he stays out of sight."

The other ducklings quickly made themselves at home. But from that moment on, everyone in the barnyard was mean to the ugly duckling. His brothers and sisters kicked him and bit him. The older ducks chased him. The hens and roosters pecked him. One day, even his mother admitted that she wished he had never been born.

When he heard that, the ugly duckling decided to run away, and he flew over the hedge and into the fields. He soon came to the marsh where the wild ducks lived, and there he fell asleep.

When he awoke, the wild ducks were standing around him, staring curiously.

"What are you?" they said. "We have never seen a duck like you before."

"I don't know myself," replied the ugly duckling shyly.

"It is only that you are so very ugly!" said the wild ducks. "But you seem nice enough, so you may stay with us if you like."

The grateful ugly duckling flew with the wild ducks over the marsh. Suddenly there were loud popping sounds. Hunters in the marsh below were firing their guns at the wild ducks! The poor ducks all dropped into the water—dead.

The ugly duckling was terrified and hid among the reeds. A hunting dog ran past him, baring his fangs. But the dog did not stop.

"Ah," the ugly duckling thought sadly. "I am so ugly that even a dog won't bite me." He sat very still until the hunters left. Then he flew alone toward the forest.

The ugly duckling flew until he was so tired that he could hardly flap his wings. It was evening by then, and a storm was gathering. Soon rain began to fall. Cold and hungry, the ugly duckling was happy to see the light of a cottage ahead. He flew toward it, and, finding the door open, he went inside.

The cottage belonged to an old woman who lived there with her big tomcat and her prize red hen. When they saw the ugly duckling, the hen began to cluck and the cat began to hiss.

"What is it?" cried the old woman, who was very nearsighted. When she caught sight of the ugly duckling she thought he was a nice fat duck who had run away from a nearby farm. "Oh, good!" she said. "Now I shall have duck's eggs to eat." She fed the ugly duckling some bread and water and told him he could stay if he liked.

This did not please the cat or the hen at all, for they liked to think that they were master and mistress of the household. After the old woman had gone to bed, they turned on the ugly duckling.

"Can you lay eggs?" clucked the hen.

"No," replied the ugly duckling.

"Can you arch your back and purr?" hissed the cat.

"No," replied the ugly duckling.

"Then what good are you?" said the cat.

"Can't you do anything at all?" said the hen.

"I can swim," replied the ugly duckling. Then he told them how lovely the water felt and what fun it was to dive to the bottom.

"Fun?" cried the hen. "Why, it sounds horrible!"

"Dreadful!" agreed the cat. "You had better learn to purr or lay eggs, or you won't be here much longer."

Then the cat scratched the ugly duckling, and the hen pecked him, until the poor creature decided he had better leave.

So the ugly duckling flew to a quiet pond in the middle of the forest. There, he could swim and dive all day long. But he was careful to hide from all the other creatures, because he had grown ashamed of his ugliness.

Autumn came. Leaves fell from the trees and the wind grew sharp. The days were growing shorter, and the nights were getting colder. It would soon be winter. It was becoming harder to find food, and the ugly duckling was hungry and lonely.

One cool evening, he was resting at the edge of the pond and gazing at the sunset, when he saw a great flock of birds flying overhead.

The birds were the most beautiful the ugly duckling had ever seen. They were white as snow with wide, strong wings and long, graceful necks. The ugly duckling did not know it, but these were swans flying south for the winter. Suddenly, they spread their wings and all together uttered a cry unlike anything the ugly duckling had ever heard. Then they flew on, their feathers gleaming in the last rays of the sun.

The ugly duckling stared after them. Then without realizing it, he arched his neck and called back to them—a cry so strange it frightened him. No living creature had ever made him feel that way before. How he wished he could be as lovely as those proud, white birds were! "But what would such royal birds say if they were to see me?" he thought sadly.

Soon cruel winter came. The ugly duckling had to swim in a circle all day to keep the pond from freezing over. Each day, the circle in which he could swim grew smaller and smaller. One day, it was so cold that, despite the ugly duckling's efforts, the pond completely froze. The poor ugly duckling could not swim another stroke, and he fell exhausted on the ice.

The next morning, a peasant passing by saw the ugly duckling lying on the ice. Feeling sorry for him, the peasant picked up the poor little bird and carried him home.

His wife put the ugly duckling next to the fire. Soon he warmed up and began to spread his wings. When the peasant's children saw this, they came running toward him, for they wanted to play with the duckling.

The ugly duckling was so frightened that he beat his wings, knocking over the milk jug. Then he flew into the butter cask and then into the barrel of cornmeal. After that, the ugly duckling looked a sight!

The woman screamed and chased him with a broom. The children fell over each other trying to catch him. The ugly duckling barely managed to escape through the window!

The rest of that winter was lonely and difficult for the ugly duckling.

Then one day, he awoke to find the warm sun shining. Green leaves were budding on the trees. Beautiful spring had come at last! Joyfully, the ugly duckling spread his wings and flew. Soon he came to a pond.

Three proud swans were gliding across the water. When the ugly duckling saw them, he felt sadder than ever. "I will swim over to those beautiful, proud birds," he thought. "I am so ugly, they will surely kill me. But it will be better to be killed by them, than be bitten by ducks and pecked by hens and hated by everyone."

So he swam toward them with his head down to show he was prepared to die. It was then that the ugly duckling saw his reflection in the water. Instead of an ugly gray bird, he was snow-white with a long graceful neck. The ugly duckling had grown into a beautiful swan!

The three swans swam to him and stroked his neck with their beaks in welcome. Just then some children came running up to the edge of the pond. "Look!" they cried. "A new swan! Why, he is the most beautiful one of all!"

The once ugly duckling shyly ruffled his feathers and thought, "When I was the ugly duckling, I never dreamed I would ever be so happy!"

THE LITTLE MERMAID

By HANS CHRISTIAN ANDERSEN

Retold by JENNIFER GREENWAY

Illustrated by ROBYN OFFICER

Deep in the blue sparkling ocean, deeper than any human has ever gone, the Sea King lived with his subjects in a splendid palace made of rare seashells and pearls.

Now, the Sea King had six beautiful mermaid daughters. The youngest one was the most beautiful. And she was much quieter and more thoughtful than her sisters. While her sisters enjoyed playing with

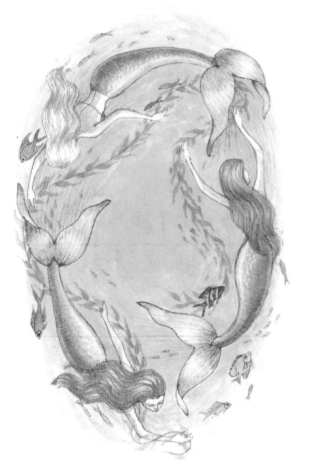

silvery fish and making wreaths of colored seaweed, the youngest found no amusement in such games. She liked more than anything to hear of the world above the sea, and she often asked her grandmother what it was like.

The little mermaid loved to hear how flowers on land had a fragrance—so different from those under the water, which had none. She was also delighted to learn that the fishes on land—for that's what grandmother called birds—sang beautiful songs. But best of all she liked to hear about the human beings who lived in the world above the waves.

When the daughters of the Sea King reached their fifteenth year, they were allowed to go to the surface of the water. But the little mermaid, being the youngest, watched all her sisters go before her.

When the oldest sister came back, she spoke of the twinkling stars. The second described a beautiful sunset. The third saw a garden full of flowers. The fourth told about the vast blue sky, and the fifth was amazed by giant pale icebergs floating in the ocean. Yet despite the wonderful sights above the water, all the little mermaid's sisters agreed that the world beneath the waves was far more beautiful.

"I shall have to see for myself," the little mermaid thought wistfully. "How I wish my turn would come."

At last, the little mermaid's fifteenth birthday came, and up she went to the world above the waves.

It was evening and the sky sparkled with silver stars. A ship lit with colored lanterns sailed toward the little mermaid. The people on board were having a party. The little mermaid swam up and peered through the window of one of the cabins.

Inside she saw a handsome prince laughing and talking with his friends. He had just turned sixteen years old, and the party was in honor of his birthday.

The little mermaid fell in love with him at once. "If only he could see me," she thought, "perhaps he would love me, too."

Just then the little mermaid saw that a terrible storm was blowing up. The waves began rising higher and higher, and the wind whistled. Soon the ship began to creak and groan. "We're going to sink!" the little mermaid heard one of the sailors yell.

Finally the ship began breaking apart, and everyone on board was cast into the water. At first, the little mermaid was glad, since now the handsome prince would be with her. Then she remembered that humans could not live underwater.

"I must save him!" the little mermaid thought. She dove again and again. At last, she found the prince deep beneath the waves. He was still alive.

She pulled him to the surface. She held his head above the water, and they drifted all night.

By dawn, the storm had passed and the little mermaid saw a quiet beach. Just beyond the beach, a white church nestled on a hill. She swam to the shore while still holding the prince and dragged him onto the sand. She kissed him on the forehead, but he did not wake up.

Then the church bell rang and a group of young women ran out of the church door. The sound of their voices frightened the little mermaid and she hid behind a rock.

One of the young women ran onto the beach and up to the prince as he was opening his eyes. She was very beautiful, and the prince smiled at her.

"You have saved my life!" he said, for he did not know it was the little mermaid who had really saved him.

Then the young woman helped the prince to his feet and led him away to the white church.

The little mermaid sighed and swam under the waves back to her father's palace. When her sisters asked her what she had seen above the waves, she would not answer. But day and night she thought of the handsome prince, and she grew sad and pale.

The little mermaid began to spend all her time roaming the world above the waves looking for the prince.

One day, she came to a beach where a large marble palace stood. To her joy, she saw the prince walking along the shore, for this palace was his.

After that the little mermaid came every day to secretly watch the prince. Her love for him grew. But she dared not show herself, because her grandmother had told her that humans were afraid of mermaids.

"They believe that everyone should have two of those props they call legs," her grandmother had said. "And they think our tails are very ugly!"

"Ah, if only I had legs," the little mermaid thought. "Perhaps then I could make the prince love me!" Then the little mermaid decided to do a terrible thing.

In the very depths of the ocean, there lived an ancient sea witch. She was wicked but very powerful. So the little mermaid went to seek her advice.

When the little mermaid entered the sea witch's cave, the sea witch stared at her and cackled. "I know why you have come, foolish princess," she said. "I can give you legs, but it will not be easy for you. You will be as graceful as you are now, but each step you take will feel as if you are treading on sharp knives!"

"I do not mind," replied the little mermaid, thinking only of the prince.

"There is more," the sea witch went on. "Once you have taken a human form, you will never be able to live with your family under the waves again. Moreover, if the prince does not love you in return and agree to marry you, you will perish. The morning after he marries another, your heart will break and you will be nothing—only the foam on the waves!"

The little mermaid turned pale. "I will still do it," she said.

"But I must be paid," said the sea witch. "In return for giving you legs I must have your voice."

The little mermaid faltered. Her voice was the loveliest of all the sea creatures, and far more beautiful than that of any mortal. "But how will I make the prince love me without my voice!" she cried.

"You are very lovely," said the witch. "Use that to charm him."

"Very well," said the little mermaid.

So the little mermaid gave her voice to the sea witch, and in return the sea witch gave her the magic potion that would make her legs.

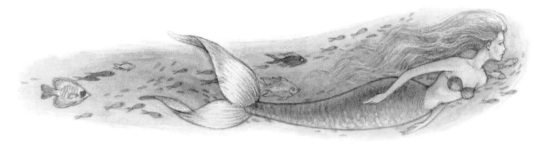

The little mermaid waited
until night and sadly bid farewell to
her sleeping father, grandmother, and
sisters. Then she swam to the beach
near the prince's palace and swallowed
the sea witch's potion.

She felt as if a sword had been passed
through her, and she fainted. When she awoke it was
morning, and to her surprise the prince was standing
over her. The little mermaid looked down and saw
that she had two pretty legs and dainty feet.

"Who are you?" the prince asked, but the little
mermaid could not answer. She was so lovely
and her blue eyes looked so sad that the
prince took pity on her and led her
to his palace.

As the sea witch had promised, every step the little mermaid took was as painful as stepping on sharp knives. But she bore it bravely.

The prince ordered his servants to dress her in fine robes. When this was done, the little mermaid was the most beautiful young woman in the palace. Yet she still could not utter a word, only stare at the prince with her sad, blue eyes.

"You poor creature," the prince said. "If only you could speak to me. You remind me of a girl I met once who saved my life when I almost drowned. She is the only woman I can ever love, but I shall never see her again. So will you stay with me instead?"

When she heard that, the little mermaid's heart almost broke. She wished she could tell the prince that it was she who had saved his life. But she could not say a word.

The prince made the little mermaid his closest companion. She did all she could to please him, but he spoke only of the one who had saved him. "I shall never see her again," he told the little mermaid. "But I am glad that you at least have been sent to me, my beautiful silent friend."

Then the little mermaid danced for him, though it hurt her terribly. She danced so gracefully the prince was enchanted and said she must stay with him always.

One day the king announced that the prince must marry the daughter of the neighboring king. The prince told the little mermaid that he would never do so. "I cannot marry that princess when I love only the girl who saved me," he said. "I would rather marry you than anyone but her." Then he kissed the little mermaid on the cheek.

The next day the king prepared a ship to travel to the nearby kingdom. The little mermaid accompanied the prince on the journey.

When the ship reached the shore, the neighboring king and the princess were there to greet them.

When the prince saw the princess, he cried, "But she is the one who saved my life! All my wishes have come true!" As soon as he was on land, he ran to the princess, leaving the little mermaid standing alone.

The princess was very beautiful and her eyes were kind and gentle. The little mermaid stared at her. "She is lovely and she seems good," the mermaid thought. "The prince loves her, for how can he know that it was I who saved his life and not she? So now I must prepare to die."

The wedding of the prince and the princess was celebrated that very night.

The prince asked the little mermaid to stand close to him during the wedding. "You must share in my happiness," he said. So the little mermaid held up the bride's veil and smiled, even though her heart was broken.

"Tomorrow I must die," she thought. "I will never see my dear sisters or my father or grandmother again!" And a tear rolled down her cheek.

Late that night the prince and his bride went to bed on the ship that was to carry them back to the prince's kingdom. Meanwhile, the little mermaid stood on the deck and gazed at the sea.

Then she saw her sisters swimming toward her. Their beautiful long hair had all been cut off. The eldest one carried a sharp knife in her hand. They were all weeping as they called to the little mermaid, "Dear sister, we gave our hair to the sea witch in exchange for this knife. Before the sun rises, you must kill the prince with it. Then your legs will disappear and your tail will grow back. After that you may come and live with us under the waves again!"

The little mermaid took the knife and went inside the ship to the prince's room. He lay there asleep beside his bride.

When she saw him, tears came to the little mermaid's eyes, and she ran to the deck and flung the knife into the sea. Then as the sun was rising, she threw herself into the water. She waited to die and become like the foam on the waves. But instead she felt herself being lifted high into the air.

"Where am I?" she cried.

"You are with us, the spirits of the air," replied a host of musical voices. "Because of your good deed, little mermaid, you have been made one of us. You will not die. Instead you will travel around the world spreading peace and kindness, and you will live with us forever."

The little mermaid felt full of joy. Looking down, she saw the prince gazing sadly into the water as if he were looking for her. She flew down to him and whispered, "Do not be sad! All is well!"

As the prince's face grew peaceful again, the little mermaid joined hands with the other spirits of the air and rose into the clouds.

Beauty *and the* Beast

Retold by SAMANTHA EASTON

Illustrated by RUTH SANDERSON

There was once a rich merchant who through no fault of his own lost his entire fortune. All he had left was a small house in the country where he and his family would now have to live.

The merchant had three daughters. The youngest was so lovely that everyone called her Beauty.

The merchant had always given his daughters the best of everything, and the two eldest girls were very spoiled. They hated their new home and did nothing but complain about it. Beauty, however, tried to make the best of things.

A year had passed in this way when the merchant received some good news. One of his ships, which he had believed lost, had come into port with all its cargo safe and sound.

Beauty's sisters were overjoyed. They were sure the family would soon be as rich as before. As their father prepared to leave for town, they begged him to bring them back fine silk dresses and jeweled necklaces.

But Beauty asked for nothing.

The merchant noticed her silence. "How about you, Beauty? What would you like?"

"I only wish you to come home safely, Father," the girl replied.

"But there must be something I can bring you," said Beauty's father.

"Very well," she said. "Bring me a rose. None grow here, and I am so fond of them."

So the merchant set off for town. When he arrived he learned that all the cargo had been stolen. There was nothing for him to do but turn around and head home.

When the merchant was only a few miles from home, a terrible storm blew up. The snow fell so heavily that the merchant could not go on. He looked for shelter, but there was none in the forest. He was growing desperate when he spotted a path through the trees. He steered his horse onto it.

As he went down the path the snow cleared and the air grew warmer. Soon the merchant was on a paved road. On either side were orange trees heavy with ripe fruit. "How strange!" he thought. He kept going until he came to a white marble palace.

The gates were open and the palace was entirely lit. The merchant wandered through the rooms, but he could find no one at home. He stopped in a room with a blazing fire. Thinking the fire must have been made for someone who would soon appear, he sat down before it and fell asleep.

The merchant awoke in the morning to find a full breakfast set out for him. He hungrily devoured it, then walked through the palace once again looking for his mysterious host. But he could find no one. Finally he decided to be on his way and went outside to find his horse.

In the garden the merchant saw a rose bush covered with beautiful flowers. "At least, I can bring Beauty her gift," he thought as he plucked one.

Then, a terrible voice above him said, "Thief! Is this how you repay the Beast's kindness? That rose will cost you your life!"

The merchant turned to see a fearsome beast looming over him. "Please forgive me, sir," he cried, falling to his knees. "I only wished to bring a rose to my daughter, Beauty." Then he told the Beast his story.

When the merchant had finished, the Beast said, "Very well, I will spare your life, but one of your daughters must agree to take your place!"

The merchant was horrified. But he accepted the condition, and the Beast let him go still carrying the rose for Beauty.

When the merchant reached home, his daughters eagerly ran to meet him. He gave them the sad news that he was as poor as ever. Then he handed Beauty her rose. "Here is what you asked for," he sighed, "but you cannot imagine what it cost!"

His daughters asked him to explain.

Upon hearing his story, the two older daughters turned on Beauty. "It is all your fault," they said. "You had to ask for a rose, and now look what you have done!"

"I know," Beauty replied. "And so it is only fair that I go to the Beast in my father's place." Her father said he would not allow her to do this, but Beauty stood firm. After a week had passed, Beauty and her father set out for the Beast's palace.

The journey passed quickly. Soon they were walking down the road lined with orange trees. Although Beauty was frightened, she could not help marveling at the Beast's gardens. They were full of fruit and flowers even though it was winter.

As before, the palace was beautifully lit, but there was no one to be seen. Inside, a fire blazed in the same room, and a big meal had been set out. But Beauty and her father were both too upset to eat. After a while, the door opened and in walked the Beast.

The Beast was horrible to look at, but Beauty greeted him politely. He asked her if she had come willingly, and she replied in a steady voice, "Yes, Beast."

The Beast then told the merchant to go home, and he gave him two chests of gold to take with him. Beauty and her father thought they would never see each other again. They embraced and the merchant reluctantly rode away.

Beauty expected the Beast to kill her at once, but he left her alone. When it grew dark, Beauty found herself before a room with her name written above it in gold letters.

The room had a graceful bed and a matching dressing table. The wardrobe was full of lovely gowns. "Surely, the Beast would not give me these things if he meant to kill me," Beauty thought. Then, feeling much better, she fell asleep.

The next morning, Beauty awoke to find breakfast set out for her. All day long she amused herself by wandering through the palace. Sometimes she heard music and voices, but she saw no one.

When evening came Beauty found a delicious supper waiting for her in her room. She was just sitting down to eat, when the Beast knocked at her door. "Beauty," he said softly. "May I please watch you eat?"

Beauty trembled with fear, but she replied bravely, "Yes, Beast."

So the Beast sat beside her, and they spoke of many things. To Beauty's surprise, the Beast was a pleasant companion. But at the end of the meal, the Beast asked, "Do you love me, Beauty? Will you marry me?"

"How can I answer?" Beauty said.

"Tell the truth," replied the Beast.

"Then, no, dear Beast," Beauty replied gently. "I cannot marry you."

"Very well," the Beast said sadly.

Every night the Beast asked Beauty the same question. And even though she refused him, he treated her very kindly.

Soon Beauty began to enjoy living in the palace. Whenever she wished for anything—some embroidery thread or a kitten to keep her company—her wish was granted at once. She also grew very fond of the Beast, who was kind and generous to her. Despite his dreadful appearance, Beauty looked forward to the evenings when he would sit with her.

Yet Beauty missed her family, especially her dear father, and she slowly grew pale and ill from longing. At last, the Beast asked her what was wrong.

"I only wish I could see my family again, dear Beast," Beauty replied.

The Beast sighed. "If you go," he said mournfully, "it will be the death of me!"

"But I will only go for a month," Beauty promised. "Then I will come back and stay with you always."

"Then go," said the Beast. "But be sure to keep your promise or you will find me dead."

The Beast gave Beauty a silver ring and told her to put it on that night and wish she were home. "Tomorrow morning you will be there," the Beast said. "And when you wish to come back to me, put the ring on your finger when you go to bed. Then turn it once, and say, 'I wish to be with my dear Beast again.' By morning you will be here."

That night Beauty filled a trunk with gifts for her father and sisters. Then she put on the ring and wished herself home.

The next morning she was there. Her father was overjoyed. Her sisters pretended they were, too. But secretly they were jealous of Beauty, because the Beast had given her many expensive and beautiful things.

One day Beauty carelessly told them that she had promised the Beast to return in a month. "Let us make her stay longer," said one of her sisters. "Then the Beast may get angry with her and not let her come back."

When it came time for Beauty to go, her sisters burst into tears. "If you leave, we shall die of grief," they wailed. So Beauty stayed one day and then another and another, but she began to worry about the Beast.

One night, Beauty had a terrible dream. In it the Beast appeared before her and said, "Beauty, you broke your promise and now I shall die!"

Terrified, Beauty woke with a start. She placed the ring on her finger, turned it once, and said, "I wish to be back with my dear Beast again."

The next morning Beauty was in the Beast's palace. All day she waited for evening when the Beast would visit her. But evening came, and the Beast did not appear.

Beauty ran through the palace calling his name, to no avail. Next, she ran into the garden. There, she saw the Beast lying very still beneath the rose bushes.

Beauty ran to him. "He is dead," she sobbed, "and it is all because of me!" Just then the Beast's eyes opened. "Oh, Beast!" Beauty cried. "I am so glad you are still alive. I never knew how much I loved you until this moment!"

"Can you really love an ugly beast like myself?" the Beast asked.

"Yes," Beauty replied.

"Will you marry me, Beauty?"

"Yes, I will, dear Beast!"

Then there was a bright flash of light, and the Beast vanished. In his place stood a handsome prince. He told Beauty he had been placed under a spell by a wicked fairy. He was doomed to remain in the form of a hideous beast until some maiden should fall in love with him. Beauty's love had broken the spell, and now the prince wished to marry her.

The prince took Beauty back to the palace and introduced her to his mother and father, who under the wicked fairy's spell had been invisible.

Then Beauty sent for her father and her sisters. She told them of the prince's spell and the coming wedding. And so the marriage of Beauty and her prince was celebrated with great joy, and they lived happily ever after.

THE LITTLE MATCH GIRL

By HANS CHRISTIAN ANDERSEN

Retold by SAMANTHA EASTON

Illustrated by ERIN AUGENSTINE

It was the last night of the year, and it was a
very cold, dark night. The streets were empty.
Everyone was home in their warm houses, busily
cooking their New Year's Eve feast of roast goose and
chestnut stuffing and apple pie and other good
things.

Though it was very late, a little girl could be seen
still walking slowly down the icy streets.

She had no hat on her head nor any shoes on her feet. When she left her house that morning, she had been wearing a pair of old slippers that were full of holes. They were far too big for her, and they had fallen off as she ran across the street to get out of the way of an oncoming carriage. One of them had vanished altogether, and a little boy had run off with the other one, saying it was so large, it would make a fine boat for his tin soldiers.

Since then, the little girl had had to go barefoot, and her little feet were blue with cold.

In her ragged apron, the little girl carried matches, and she held a packet of them in her hand. She was supposed to be selling them, but no one had bought a single match from her all day or given her so much as a copper penny. Now, the child was shivering and faint with hunger as she walked forlornly through the darkness.

Sometimes, she stopped to stare into the lighted windows of the houses along the streets. All the houses were decorated in honor of the New Year. Delicious smells wafted out to the street, making the little girl feel hungrier.

At last, she came to a corner between two tall stone houses that was sheltered from the icy wind.

The little girl sat down there and pulled her feet under her, hoping to warm them. But it did no good. The cold air seemed to sink into her very bones.

The little girl was afraid to go home, for she had not sold any matches that day. She knew her father would probably beat her for that. Besides, it was not much warmer at home than it was outside in the street—the walls of their rooms were so full of holes.

Her mother had tried to stuff them with straw and rags, but the wind howled through them as strong as ever.

The little girl stretched out her hands. They were stiff with cold. "If I lit just one of these matches," she thought, "I would feel so much warmer!" She gazed longingly at the packet of matches in her hand.

Then she drew one out and struck it against the wall, making a loud scratch. The match sputtered and flared, casting a bright, clear light.

The little girl stared at it. All of a sudden, it seemed to her that she was sitting in front of a big iron stove with feet of brightly polished brass. Inside, a coal fire blazed brightly.

How warm and beautiful that fire was! Eagerly, the little girl stretched out her hands toward it. She pulled out her little bare feet to warm them by the glowing embers of the wonderful fire. But just then, the match went out.

The big iron stove vanished, and the little girl found herself on the cold, dark street again, holding a half-burned match in her hand.

The little girl pulled out another match and struck it. The flame rose, casting a light on the stone wall beside her. Suddenly the walls looked as transparent as glass.

It seemed to the child that she could see right through the wall into a room. There was a long table covered with a snow-white cloth and set with fine china, crystal glasses, and silver forks and knives and spoons. In the center, an enormous platter held a steaming roast goose stuffed with apples and sausage. How delicious it looked!

Then, something even more wonderful happened. The goose leaped off the platter, and with a knife and fork still stuck in its breast, came walking toward the little girl. She reached out her hands toward it. But as she did so the match went out.

Once again everything turned dark, and the little girl found herself staring only at the damp stone wall.

As quickly as she could, she pulled out another match and struck it.

This time the light blazed forth even more brightly, and the little girl found herself gazing up at an enormous Christmas tree.

It was much larger and more splendidly decorated than any Christmas tree she had ever seen. Even the ones she had glimpsed through the windows of rich people's houses could not compare with it.

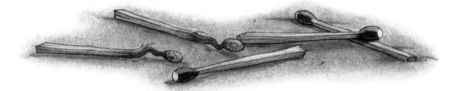

Hundreds upon hundreds of lit candles gleamed in its green branches. Colored pictures of angels hung from it—pictures such as those the little girl had sometimes seen in shop windows at Christmastime. Only these pictures were even more lifelike and far more beautiful.

The child stretched out her hand toward the tree. Just then the match flickered out. But as the little girl watched, the candles on the Christmas tree seemed to rise higher and higher, until she realized she was staring at the stars in the sky.

They twinkled down at her so brightly and looked so beautiful she felt as if her heart would break. Then she saw one of them fall, leaving a bright trail of light behind it.

"Somebody must be dying," the little girl thought. Her grandmother, the one person in the world who had ever truly loved her, had once told her that whenever a star falls it means a soul is rising to heaven.

The little girl pulled out another match and struck it against the wall. This time, the light flared up in front of her, forming a bright circle like a halo.

In the center of it stood the little girl's grandmother. She looked so radiant and loving that the little girl could not help but cry out to her.

"Oh, Grandmother," she said. "Please take me with you. I know that when the match goes out you will vanish, just like the big warm stove and the lovely roast goose and the beautiful Christmas tree. Oh, Grandmother, please don't leave me here. Don't, please!"

And as the match burned out, the little girl desperately clutched the packet and struck the rest of the matches against the hard stone wall. They burst

into flame, and together they made a light that
seemed brighter than the noonday sun.

In the blazing light, the little girl saw her grandmother again. The little girl stretched out her hands,
and her grandmother gently took the child in her arms.

Then together they rose high above the dark icy
streets to a place where there was no more hunger, no
more cold, and no more pain or suffering. They rose
all the way to heaven.

Early the next morning some passersby came upon the little match girl.

She was still sitting in the corner between the two houses, leaning against the wall. She was smiling but her small cheeks were pale, for she had frozen to death during the night. "Oh, the poor child," the people mourned.

Some of the people pointed at the bundle of burnt matches the child held in her hand. "Look!" they said. "The little creature must have tried to warm herself!"

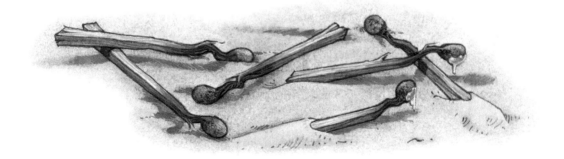

But they could not possibly know all the wonders the little match girl had seen that night. Nor would anyone know how joyfully she and her grandmother had celebrated the coming of the New Year.

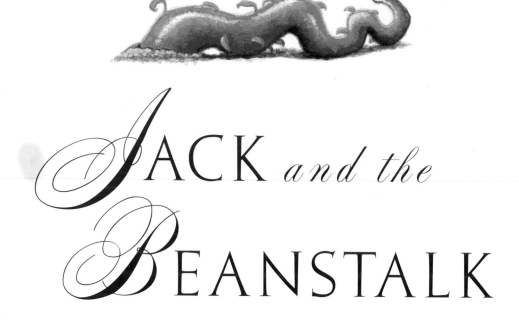

JACK *and the* BEANSTALK

Retold by JENNIFER GREENWAY

Illustrated by RICHARD BERNAL

Once upon a time there was a widow who lived in a tumbledown cottage with her son Jack. Jack and his mother were so poor that all they had was an old white cow.

One day when there was no food in the house, and no money to buy any, the widow said to herself, "I will have to sell our cow, or Jack and I will surely starve."

So Jack's mother called him to her and said, "I want you to take the cow to market and sell her. But be sure you get a good price, for she is all we have."

"Yes, Mother," Jack replied, and he put a collar on the cow and headed to town.

Jack was delighted to be going to market by himself. As he walked he whistled a cheerful tune.

He was interrupted when he heard someone say, "You seem to be in a fine mood, young man. Where are you going today?"

Jack turned around. On the side of the road stood a strange little man. He was about four feet tall and dressed in a bright green suit.

"Why, I'm off to market," Jack said, "to sell our old cow."

"I'll buy your cow, if you'd like," said the little man.

"What will you give me for her?" asked Jack.

"I'll give you these magic beans," the little man replied. Then he opened his hand. Jack looked at the beans in the man's palm. They were all the colors of the rainbow.

"Magic beans!" Jack cried. "I've never seen any before!" And he traded the cow for the beautiful magic beans.

"Mother will be so happy," Jack thought, feeling very pleased with himself. Then he ran home as fast as he could to show her the magic beans.

But Jack's mother was not happy when she learned what he had done.

"Oh, Jack," she cried. "How could you be so stupid! You traded our cow for a handful of beans!" Jack's mother was so angry, she picked up the magic beans and threw them out the window.

Jack realized his mistake, but it was too late. The cow was gone and there was still nothing to eat for supper. Jack went to bed, feeling very foolish.

All night, Jack tossed and turned. "My poor mother and I will have nothing to eat tomorrow either," he thought miserably. "And it is all because of me and those magic beans!"

The next morning, Jack gloomily climbed out of bed. When he went to the window, he saw an amazing sight.

Where his mother had thrown the magic beans, a giant beanstalk was growing. It was thick and tall—so tall that it reached into the clouds!

"Mother, come quickly!" Jack called. And together they stood in the garden, staring in wonder at the beanstalk.

"I wonder where it goes," Jack said. "Perhaps I'll climb it and find out!"

"You'll do no such thing," said his mother. "Those beans have already caused enough trouble!"

But it was too late, for Jack had already started up the beanstalk. Up he climbed, higher and higher, until the cottage below looked no bigger than a bird's nest. Still, Jack could not see to the top of the beanstalk.

At last, Jack climbed through the clouds. There he found himself at the top of the beanstalk. A field of clouds stretched in every direction. In the distance, Jack could see an enormous stone castle.

He jumped off the beanstalk and walked toward the castle. Soon he stood before the entrance—a huge iron door. Not knowing what else to do, Jack pulled the bell. After a moment, the great door slowly swung open.

To Jack's horror, there stood a huge, ugly giantess looking down at him. Before Jack could run away, the giantess scooped him up in her huge hand. "Oh, good!" she said in a great big voice. "I've been looking for someone to help me with my chores."

Jack was so frightened, all he could say was, "Of course. What do you want me to do?"

"Well," said the giantess. "First you may help me light the fire and polish the boots. Now, we must be very careful when my husband comes home, for there is nothing he likes better than to eat roasted Englishmen for dinner!"

Jack didn't like the sound of that. But the giantess promised that she would hide Jack in the cupboard when her husband came. So he helped her light the fire and polish her boots.

All of a sudden, Jack heard a terrible sound like the roaring of thunder.

"That's my husband," the giantess cried, and she quickly hid Jack in the cupboard. Then Jack heard a great booming voice:

Fe, fi, fo, fum!
I smell the blood of an Englishman.
Be he alive or be he dead
I'll grind his bones to make my bread!

And in stomped the giant.

He was much bigger than his wife and much uglier, too. He sat down at the table and shouted, "I smell an Englishman. Catch him and roast him at once!"

"Don't be silly," replied his wife. "That's only the mutton stew I've cooked for your supper." Peering through the keyhole of the cupboard, Jack watched her set down the biggest bowl of mutton stew he had ever seen.

The bowl of stew was so big that Jack could have sailed one of his small boats across it. The giant quickly ate the stew. He called for another bowl, and ate that too.

When he was finished, the giant said to his wife, "Now bring me the goose that lays the golden eggs." His wife brought a very ordinary-looking goose and set it before the giant. Then she went to bed.

After she was gone, the giant turned to the goose and said, "Lay!" The goose promptly laid an egg of pure gold. "Lay!" the giant said a second time, and the goose laid another golden egg. "Lay!" the giant commanded a third time, and the goose laid a third egg of gold.

Jack's eyes grew wide as he watched through the keyhole. "A goose that lays golden eggs!" he thought to himself. "Why, that would be a fine thing to have!" Jack wondered how he might steal it.

After a time, the giant's eyelids began to grow heavy and soon he fell asleep right at the table. He snored so loudly that the walls of the castle shook.

When Jack was quite sure that the giant was fast asleep, he crept out of the cupboard and tiptoed across the table. Then he snatched the goose that laid the golden eggs.

With the magic goose under his arm, Jack
leaped off the table and ran across the stone floor
toward the door. Just as he reached it, however,
the terrified goose cried, "Help! I'm being stolen.
Help!"

The giant awoke with a start. When he spotted
Jack with the goose, he came racing after them!

"Stop," the giant shouted. "Stop, thief! Give me back my goose!"

But Jack didn't stop. He was too frightened to turn around. He kept running as fast as he could across the clouds to the giant beanstalk.

At last, he saw the top of the beanstalk. And still clutching the magic goose, he started climbing down the beanstalk. But he had not gone far, when the beanstalk began to sway violently.

Looking up, Jack saw that the giant was coming down the beanstalk after him! Jack began to climb down faster. The giant began climbing down faster, too. Just as the giant was about to catch up with him, Jack reached the bottom of the beanstalk.

He saw his mother standing by the cottage door, and he called to her, "Mother, quick! Fetch me the axe!"

His mother came running with the axe. Jack grabbed it and, with a single blow, chopped through the beanstalk.

With a great groan, the beanstalk came crashing down, and the giant fell with it. Now, where the giant landed no one knows, but Jack and his mother never saw him again.

Jack showed his mother the goose that laid the golden eggs, and she fed it some dried corn. The goose was so happy to be free from the giant that it laid a golden egg, then another, and another. Jack took the golden eggs to market and traded them for food and a new cow and much more besides.

And ever after Jack had climbed that giant beanstalk, he and his mother and the goose that laid the golden eggs all lived happily together.

LITTLE RED
RIDING HOOD

By THE BROTHERS GRIMM

Retold by JENNIFER GREENWAY

Illustrated by ELIZABETH MILES

There once lived a girl whose name was Little Red Riding Hood. She was called that because she always wore a red velvet cloak and hood that her grandmother had made for her.

Now her grandmother had been feeling ill, and one day Little Red Riding Hood's mother said to her, "I want you to take this basket of cakes and honey to Granny."

"Now go straight to Granny's," her mother told her, "and be sure you don't speak to any strangers on the way, and whatever you do, don't stray from the path!" Little Red Riding Hood promised to do as she was told.

Her grandmother lived on the other side of a great forest. So, Little Red Riding Hood went skipping quickly down the path with her basket under her arm.

She had not gone far when she met a big wolf.

"Good morning, Little Red Riding Hood," said the wolf. "Where are you going in such a hurry?"

Little Red Riding Hood did not know what a wicked creature the wolf was, so she replied politely, "I am going to see my grandmother. She has been ill, and I am bringing her this basket of cakes and honey."

"How nice," said the wolf. But to himself he thought, "What good luck! If I am clever I can have both Little Red Riding Hood and her grandmother for supper!"

Then he smiled at Little Red Riding Hood and said, "How lovely the woods look today! What a pity you have to rush on such a beautiful morning!"

Little Red Riding Hood looked around. Sunbeams were dancing in the trees, and bright flowers were waving their heads in the breeze. "I'm sure Grandmother would love a bouquet of flowers," she thought. "It's so early that surely I can stop for just a few minutes and pick some."

So Little Red Riding Hood left the path and skipped into the woods to pick flowers. Meanwhile the wolf ran as fast as he could to Grandmother's house.

When the wolf reached Grandmother's house, he knocked on the door.

"Who's there?" called Little Red Riding Hood's grandmother.

"It is I, Little Red Riding Hood!" said the wolf, disguising his voice. "I've brought you a basket of cakes and honey."

"I am too sick to get out of bed," Grandmother replied. "But the door is open, Little Red Riding Hood, just let yourself in and come up to my bedroom."

So the wicked wolf pushed open the door, came inside and climbed the stairs to Grandmother's bedroom. Then he went to Grandmother's bed and gobbled up the old woman!

Then the wicked wolf pulled one of
Grandmother's flannel nightgowns over his head,
even though it was much too small for him. Next, he
put on Grandmother's warm woolen dressing gown.
He even took Grandmother's spectacles and stuck
them on the end of his long nose.

Then the wolf looked at himself in the mirror. He
didn't look anything like Grandmother. And his long
ears were showing. So the wolf put on Grandmother's
lace nightcap, to try to hide them.

Then he climbed into Grandmother's bed, drew
the covers over his nose, and settled back to wait for
Little Red Riding Hood.

Meanwhile Little Red Riding Hood was still in the woods picking flowers. Every time she picked one, she seemed to see a prettier one just a little ways off. And so she strayed farther and farther from the path.

When she had picked so many flowers that she could not hold even one more, she returned to the path and headed again for Grandmother's house.

When Little Red Riding Hood arrived, she was surprised to find the door open.

"Hello," she called. "Grandmother, it's me."

"Just come in!" came Grandmother's voice. "I am too ill to get out of bed!"

How strange her grandmother's voice sounded. "She must be very ill," thought Little Red Riding Hood. So the little girl ran up the stairs to her grandmother's bedroom.

Little Red Riding Hood stood beside her grandmother's bed. How strange her grandmother looked!

"Why, Grandmother," she said. "What big ears you have!"

"All the better to hear you with, my dear," said the wolf.

"But, Grandmother, what big eyes you have!" said Little Red Riding Hood.

"All the better to see you with, my dear," said the wolf.

"But, Grandmother, what big hands you have!" said Little Red Riding Hood.

"All the better to hug you with, my dear," said the wolf.

"But, Grandmother," said Little Red Riding Hood. "What big teeth you have!"

"All the better to eat you with, my dear," said the wolf.

And with that the wicked wolf jumped out of the bed and opened his jaws wide.

"Why, you're not Grandmother!" cried Little Red Riding Hood.

"No, I'm not," said the wolf. "And I'm going to eat you up!"

Then the wolf snapped at Little Red Riding Hood and swallowed her in a single gulp!

After that, the wolf felt full. He rubbed his belly contentedly. "That was a good meal," he said, and then he started to yawn. "Now I could do with a nap!"

So the wolf climbed back into Grandmother's bed. Then he pulled the covers over his head and closed his eyes.

Soon the wolf was fast asleep and he began to snore very loudly. He snored so loudly that all the windows in Grandmother's house rattled.

Toward evening, a huntsman came walking by and heard the wolf snoring.

"That is strange," he thought to himself. "The old woman is snoring awfully loudly! I wonder if she is all right."

So the huntsman walked up to Grandmother's house. To his great surprise the door was wide open. "Hello! Hello!" called the huntsman. "Is anybody home?"

But there was no answer. The wicked wolf was sleeping too soundly to hear the huntsman.

"I'll just go in and make sure everything is all right," the huntsman thought. So he went inside and tiptoed up the stairs.

As he climbed the stairs, the snoring grew louder and louder. The huntsman followed the snoring all the way to Grandmother's bed.

The huntsman looked at Grandmother's bed and saw the wolf lying fast asleep.

"Ah-ha," said the huntsman. "So it's you who is snoring so loudly, you rascal! I've been hunting for you for a long time, and now it looks as if I've got you!"

The huntsman raised his gun and was about to shoot the wolf when it occurred to him that the wolf might have eaten the old woman.

So the huntsman took a knife and cut open the wolf. Out stepped Little Red Riding Hood and her grandmother. They were both happy to be saved.

Then the huntsman filled the wolf's stomach with heavy stones and sewed it up. When the wolf awoke and saw the huntsman, he tried to run away. But the stones were so heavy that he fell down dead!

Then the huntsman, Little Red Riding Hood, and Grandmother ate all the delicious cakes and honey that Little Red Riding Hood had brought.

Soon Grandmother was feeling well again, and Little Red Riding Hood started home.

When she returned, Little Red Riding Hood told her mother everything that had happened. "Never again will I speak to strangers or stray from the path when you have told me not to!" she said.

Her mother hugged her tight. "I'm sure you won't," she said, and Little Red Riding Hood never did!

THUMBELINA

By HANS CHRISTIAN ANDERSEN

Retold by JENNIFER GREENWAY

Illustrated by ROBYN OFFICER

There once lived a couple who longed to have a child, but their wish did not come true. At last, the woman went to a fairy and asked for her help. The fairy gave her a seed and said, "Plant this in a flower-pot and water it carefully."

Soon a beautiful flower sprang up. It looked like a tulip with its petals tightly closed.

"How lovely," said the woman, kissing the flower. As she did so, the petals opened. Inside sat a tiny, graceful girl no bigger than the woman's thumb. The woman was overjoyed. She and her husband named the child Thumbelina.

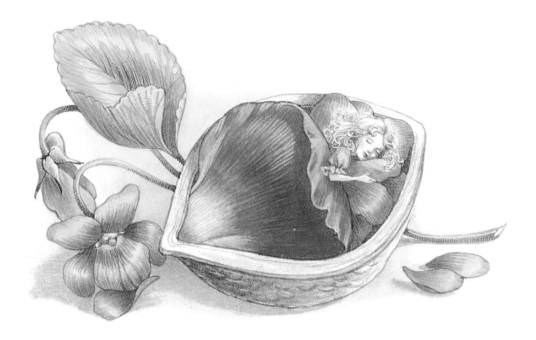

Thumbelina's cradle was a walnut shell. She had a pillow of violets and a quilt of rose petals. At night her cradle sat on the windowsill. During the day, the woman kept a bowl filled with water on the table. Thumbelina amused herself by rowing around the bowl in a boat made of a large tulip petal. She used two white horsehairs for oars. As she rowed, she sang in the tiniest, prettiest voice imaginable.

One night a big ugly toad hopped through the window. When the toad saw Thumbelina asleep in her cradle, she cried, "She would make the perfect wife for my son!"

The ugly toad snatched the cradle with Thumbelina inside and carried it to her home in the swamp.

The toad set Thumbelina on a large lily pad in the middle of the water so she could not escape. Then she went to fetch her son, who was even bigger and uglier than she was.

While the toad was gone, Thumbelina woke up. When she saw where she was, she began to cry and wonder how she would ever get home again. Some fish swimming below heard Thumbelina's cries.

When the fish saw how pretty Thumbelina was, they felt sorry for her. "We must set her free," they said, "so she does not have to marry the toad's son." The little fish began to bite at the stem of the lily

pad. Before long, they had gnawed through it, and the lily pad floated away.

Just then the toad returned with her son. "Stop!" the son called after Thumbelina. "Where are you going? You are to be my wife and live with me here in the swamp!" But it was too late. Thumbelina was already floating downstream.

Thumbelina went a long way, past wide green fields and deep shady woods. Birds and butterflies stopped to say hello to her, and she felt very happy.

Suddenly, a big brown beetle swooped down and seized Thumbelina in his claws. "How pretty you are!" he said. "I shall make you my wife!" How frightened Thumbelina was, but there was nothing she could do!

The beetle sat her on the branch of a tall tree to show her to the other beetles. But they did not think Thumbelina was pretty at all. "How ugly she is!" they sneered, turning up their feelers. "Her waist is so slim, and she has only two legs! She looks horrible!"

After that, the beetle decided he didn't want Thumbelina for a wife after all. So he flew her down from the tree and set her on a daisy.

Thumbelina was very sad, since she felt the beetles were right. She did not know that she was really very lovely.

All summer Thumbelina lived in the forest. She wove herself a bed of grass and hung it under a large leaf to shelter herself from the rain. She drank the morning dew and ate nectar from the flowers. She was perfectly content until autumn came—and then winter.

First, the leaf Thumbelina lived under died and
shriveled. Now she had no shelter from the wind and
rain. There was no longer any food to eat, either.
Then it began to snow, and Thumbelina almost froze
to death. So she went looking for food and shelter.

She walked until she came to a large cornfield.
The cornstalks had been cut long before. Nothing
was left but the stubble, which to Thumbelina
seemed as tall as a great forest. At last, she found the
home of a field mouse.

She knocked timidly on the door. When the field
mouse answered, Thumbelina said shyly, "Please, can
you spare a grain of barley?"

The field mouse, who was a kind thing, replied,
"Of course! Come in, you dear little creature!" She
led Thumbelina inside and fed her.

The field mouse's home was very comfortable, and her cupboards were full of the food she had stored for winter. So she told Thumbelina, "If you will keep my house tidy for me and tell me some good stories, you may stay with me all winter, if you like."

"Yes, please!" cried Thumbelina. And so she did all that the field mouse asked, and in return she was kept warm and well fed.

One day the field mouse said, "Listen, Thumbelina. My neighbor is coming to pay us a visit tomorrow. He is much richer than I, and he wears a beautiful black velvet coat. Oh, he is a very clever man! But he is blind, so be sure to tell him your very best stories."

"Of course," said Thumbelina. But she was not very excited about the visitor, for he was a mole.

The mole came the next day, wearing his black velvet coat. Even though he was very rich and probably very learned, as well, Thumbelina did not like him. He said dreadful things about the sun and the flowers and birds, yet he had never seen them.

Nevertheless, Thumbelina told him her best stories and sang him all the songs she knew. She had such a lovely voice that the mole fell in love with her. However, he did not say anything, because he was very cautious. Instead, he invited Thumbelina and the field mouse to pay him a visit.

So the three set out through a tunnel the mole had recently dug between his home and that of the field mouse. "Now, please watch your step," the mole told them. "It's quite dark here and there is a dead bird farther down the tunnel. But don't let that alarm you!"

When they came to the dead bird, the mole accidentally pushed his nose through the roof of the tunnel. The sun came shining through, and Thumbelina clearly saw the bird.

He was a swallow, and he did not look as if he had been dead for long. "Poor bird," Thumbelina thought sadly. "He must have died of the cold."

The mole pushed the bird aside roughly. "Useless creatures, birds!" he said gruffly. Thumbelina said nothing. But when the mole and the field mouse had gone ahead, she bent over and kissed the bird. "Perhaps you were one of the birds that sang to me all summer," she said. "How nice it was to hear your sweet music!"

After the mole showed them his house and gave them tea, he led them home again. Then he repaired the hole so no sunlight or cold could enter. But that night Thumbelina could not sleep.

She kept thinking of the poor swallow in the tunnel. At last, she crept from her bed and wove a blanket out of hay. She took it into the tunnel and laid it gently over the swallow.

Thumbelina sadly laid her head on the bird's breast. When she did, she heard a sound. It was the beating of the swallow's heart. He was not dead, only numb with cold. Thumbelina was afraid—the swallow was much bigger than she—but she bravely wrapped the blanket more tightly around him. Then she tiptoed away.

The next day she slipped away to visit the swallow again. He was awake now but very weak. So Thumbelina brought him water and honey, and all through the long cold winter she carefully nursed the swallow back to health. She told the field mouse and the mole nothing of this, for they did not think much of birds.

At last, spring came. The swallow was now well
enough to fly away. Thumbelina re-opened the hole
in the roof of the tunnel for him.

"Why don't you come with me?" the swallow
asked Thumbelina. "I can take you to warm, beautiful
places."

Thumbelina dearly wished she could go with the
swallow, but she shook her head. "The field mouse

has been very kind to me," she said, "I cannot just leave her!"

"Very well," said the swallow. "Farewell, kind maiden. I hope I see you again." And with that, the swallow flew away.

Tears filled Thumbelina's eyes. She was very fond of the swallow and would miss him so much.

Spring passed, then summer. Thumbelina worked for the field mouse, who treated her kindly but hardly ever let her go outside into the beautiful sunshine.

One day, as autumn was coming, the field mouse said to her, "I have good news, dear Thumbelina. The mole has asked for your hand in marriage. We must work to get your wedding clothes ready!"

"But I don't want to marry the mole!" cried Thumbelina, bursting into tears at the thought of living with him in his dark, underground tunnel far from the bright sun and all the lovely flowers.

"Don't be silly," the field mouse said crossly. "The mole is handsome and rich. He will make you an excellent husband. Marry him or I will bite you!"

The field mouse told Thumbelina the wedding would take place in a month. Four spiders spun the wedding veil, while Thumbelina sewed her tiny wedding gown.

As the wedding day drew near, Thumbelina became sadder and sadder. How dreadful it would be to always live in the darkness. Would she ever see the blue sky or the bright sun again? Would she ever hear a bird sing?

The day before the wedding, Thumbelina begged the field mouse to let her go outside one last time. At last, the field mouse gave her permission.

Thumbelina slipped out the door and stared longingly at the bright sky.

"Farewell, beautiful sun," she cried, stretching out her arms. "Farewell, sweet flowers! Please say hello to my dear swallow for me if you ever see him again!"

Just then Thumbelina heard a tweet, tweet above her head, and there was the swallow himself! He was flying south for winter, and he had come to say good-bye to Thumbelina before he went.

Thumbelina began to cry. She told him how she was to marry the mole the next day.

"Oh, no," cried the swallow. "Come with me instead. I will fly you to beautiful lands where the sun always shines and flowers always bloom."

"Oh, yes," Thumbelina said, "I will go with you!" for she could not bear to marry the mole.

Quickly she climbed on the swallow's back. Then the bird spread his wings and he and Thumbelina flew away. They flew over tall pine forests and snow-covered mountain peaks to warm countries where the grass is always green and orange and lemon trees grow.

After several days, they came to a clear blue lake. An ancient palace of white marble stood beside it. In the garden lay a marble pillar broken into three pieces.

Large, beautiful flowers were growing among the pieces of pillar. The swallow placed Thumbelina beside the most beautiful flower. "I think you will be happy here," he told her.

Just then the petals opened. Inside was a tiny man with shining gossamer wings. He was the fairy of that flower and king of all the flower fairies. He was just Thumbelina's size, and he fell in love with her at once.

"Will you be my wife?" he asked. Thumbelina smiled, for he was nothing like the horrible mole. "Yes," she said happily.

At that all the flowers opened and each flower fairy gave Thumbelina a gift. The best gift of all was a pair of tiny gossamer wings. Now Thumbelina would be able to fly and flit from flower to flower.

At Thumbelina's wedding to the fairy king, the swallow sang a special wedding song. Then it was time for him to fly back north. As he went he sang of Thumbelina, and that is how we came to hear her story.

Nutcracker

By E.T.A. HOFFMANN

Retold by FIONA BLACK

Illustrated by SCOTT GUSTAFSON

*I*t was Christmas Eve. The Stahlbaum family was gathered around a tall Christmas tree that was beautifully decorated with glowing candles, candied apples, and sugar almonds. The children, Fritz and Marie, were playing with their new presents when a strange little man with long white hair and a black patch over one eye entered the room.

"Godpapa Drosselmier," the children cried happily as they rushed to him. Despite his odd appearance, their godfather was very kind and clever. He could fix any watch or clock, and he had made them many remarkable toys, too.

"Merry Christmas!" said Godpapa Drosselmier as he handed each child a present. Fritz's gift was a set of tin soldiers, each carrying a handsome sword. Marie's gift was a little wooden man in a bright red uniform.

"Please take good care of this little fellow, Marie," her godfather said solemnly. "He means a great deal to me!"

Marie took the little man in her arms. Despite his elegant uniform and bright paint, he was rather ugly. His head was far too big for his body, and his mouth cut from ear to ear!

"Why, it's a nutcracker!" cried her father. Then he showed Marie how to put a nut in the little man's mouth and shut it tight. There was a quick crack, and the nutshell fell to the floor.

Marie hugged the nutcracker. "Thank you, Godpapa," she cried. "He is my favorite present!"

"How can you like such an ugly fellow?" said Fritz scornfully.

"Don't say that," cried Marie. "You'll hurt his feelings!"

"I'm afraid Fritz is right," Godpapa Drosselmier said. "Our poor nutcracker is rather ugly. If you like, I'll tell you the story of how ugliness came into his family."

"Oh, please do!" begged the children.

"Very well," began their godfather. And this is the tale he told.

Many years ago there lived a king who had a very beautiful daughter. Her name was Princess Pirlipat. She had golden hair and rosy cheeks. Her father adored her and one year he planned a great feast in honor of her birthday.

Now the king was very fond of sausages, and the queen always made them herself. So in honor of the celebration the king asked his wife to make three hundred of her best sausages.

Just as the queen had finished making them, Dame Mouserink, the queen of mice, came into the kitchen. "Let me taste a bit of sausage!" she squeaked.

"Of course," the queen replied. Then Dame Mouserink, followed by all her greedy relations, pounced on the sausages and ate them all up!

When the king learned what had happened he was furious. He announced that whoever rid the kingdom of mice would win the princess's hand in marriage.

Now, one of the king's closest advisors was a clever clockmaker. This clockmaker had a nephew. The boy had been orphaned as a baby and raised by the clockmaker. The nephew was a charming, handsome young man and had the remarkable ability of cracking even the hardest nuts with his teeth. Everyone called him "The Handsome Nutcracker."

The clockmaker decided it would be a fine thing if his nephew married the beautiful Princess Pirlipat. So he began to plan the world's first mousetrap. He baited his traps with sausage. Then he had his nephew set the traps throughout the palace. All of Dame Mouserink's greedy relatives were soon trapped and put to death. But Dame

Mouserink herself was far too clever to become caught in such a way.

Nevertheless, the king was overjoyed and summoned the clockmaker's nephew. With great fanfare he announced that the boy could one day marry the lovely princess.

No sooner had he spoken than Dame Mouserink appeared and made this pronouncement:

I, queen of mice, pronounce this curse:

The Handsome Nutcracker shall become
hideously ugly.
And for him I predict the worst:

My son, the mouse with seven crowns,
Will surely bring the Nutcracker down!

The king's soldiers quickly fell on Dame
Mouserink and killed her. Then Princess Pirlipat
looked at the clockmaker's nephew and shrieked,
"Oh, how ugly he is! I will never marry him!" You
see, the clockmaker's handsome nephew had
changed. He now had a
huge misshapen head.

The clockmaker was heartbroken and felt he was to blame for his nephew's misfortune. So he visited a famous astrologer to learn how the spell might be broken.

"Do not despair," the astrologer reported after studying the boy's stars. "Your nephew is such a fine young man that he will win a kingdom of his own. But unless he defeats Dame Mouserink's son—the Mouse with Seven Crowns—and wins a lady's heart despite his ugliness, he will never return to his proper form."

"And so," finished Godpapa Drosselmier, "now you know how the mousetrap was invented and why nutcrackers are so ugly."

"What was the clever clockmaker's name?" asked Fritz.

His Godpapa smiled strangely. "Drosselmier," he replied. "Just like mine."

By now it had grown late, and Mrs. Stahlbaum told the children it was time to put their new toys away and go to bed.

Fritz quickly put his soldiers in the toy cabinet in the corner of the room and climbed the stairs to his bedroom. But Marie begged to stay up a little while longer. "I want to put my nutcracker to bed properly," she explained.

After everyone else had gone to bed, the sitting room seemed dark and mysterious. Marie stared into the nutcracker's painted blue eyes. They had such a sad expression that she wondered if her Godpapa's story could be true. "Don't worry, dear nutcracker," she whispered. "I will help you if I can!"

Then the room filled with rustling and rattling noises. Startled, Marie looked around. The clock, which had started to strike the hour, whirred to a stop. Then Marie heard a voice say:

Clocks, listen and stop your ticking.
Now the mouse king is awakening.
In the light of the full moon
Comes the hour of the nutcracker's doom!

At that, hundreds of mice began squeezing through all the cracks in the wall and floor.

They organized themselves into troops and marched in place. Then the floor cracked open and from the crack rose a horrible creature—a mouse with seven heads. The seven heads grew from one huge body, and each was topped by a shining crown. The seven heads called the mouse army to order, and they began marching toward the toy cabinet!

Marie was terrified, but then she heard another voice cry:

Awake! For the hour has come
When we must fight for our kingdom.
Come, toys, and follow me,
The nutcracker calls to
thee!

Then the nutcracker came marching out of the cabinet with his sword drawn. Marie's dolls and Fritz's tin soldiers leaped down from their shelves in the cabinet and followed him. They were joined by the teddy bears, the puppets, and the stuffed cotton clown.

With the nutcracker leading, the toys bravely advanced toward the mouse king's army. Fritz's tin soldiers loaded their cannons with lemon drops and hazelnuts and fired at the mice. But little by little the mice gained the advantage. They bit the puppets and the stuffed cotton clown and knocked over Fritz's tin soldiers. They soon surrounded the nutcracker.

"Prepare to meet your doom!" squealed the mouse king's seven heads as he scurried toward the nutcracker.

Marie's heart was beating so fast she thought she would faint. But she knew she had to do something to save her friend. So she took off her shoe and threw it at the mouse king.

Then everything around her seemed to grow dark and she fell to the floor.

When Marie opened her eyes, all traces of the battle had vanished. The nutcracker stood beside her holding his sword in one hand and the mouse king's seven crowns in the other.

"Dear Miss Stahlbaum," he said, "thanks to your courage I was saved from certain death. Please come with me. I have marvelous things to show you!" Then he helped Marie to her feet and opened the door of the toy cabinet.

To her amazement Marie found that she was small
enough to step inside the toy cabinet. A bright light
washed over her. Then she found herself in a meadow
that glittered with a rainbow of colors. "This is
Candy Meadow," the nutcracker said. "We are in my
kingdom, which is called Toyland."

He led Marie through a gate made of raisins
and almonds and down a road of brightly colored
hard candies. Soon they were in a gingerbread town
where gingerbread men and women waved at them
as they passed.

They came to another town. This one was made of spun sugar and dainty china and glass people sang to them.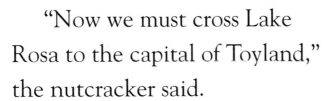

"Now we must cross Lake Rosa to the capital of Toyland," the nutcracker said.

As he spoke, Marie saw a beautiful rose-colored lake and on it there was a little gold boat pulled by dolphins.

She and the nutcracker stepped into the boat and were soon pulled across the lake. Ahead, Marie could see a beautiful city made of sugar plums and candied fruits. But most wonderful of all was a lofty castle with tall rose-colored spires.

"This is my home, Marzipan Castle," said the nutcracker.

Elegantly dressed little dolls greeted them, "Hail
to the King of Toyland!" Up until then Marie had
been too dazzled by everything she saw to say a word.
But now she turned to the nutcracker and cried,
"Then Godpapa's story is true, and you are his
nephew!"

"Yes," replied the nutcracker. "With your help, I have defeated the mouse king and won back my kingdom, and yet . . ." He sighed so sorrowfully that Marie was sure he must be thinking of the lovely Princess Pirlipat, who had refused his hand.

"I don't understand why the princess was so mean," Marie said, feeling very sorry for the nutcracker. "I would have remained your friend and companion no matter what you looked like. I would not have minded one bit if you were in the shape of a nutcracker!"

As soon as Marie had spoken, a strange thing happened. The castle around her wavered and then disappeared, and Marie felt as if she were falling and falling.

When she landed she was lying in her own bed, and her mother was standing over her. "Wake up, Sleepy Head," Mother said. "It is Christmas morning."

"Oh, Mother," Marie said. "So much has happened!" And she told her mother about the nutcracker and the mouse king and her visit to Toyland.

"You have had a long, beautiful dream," her mother said. "But now you must get up. We have

visitors. Godpapa Drosselmier is here with his nephew."

Marie quickly dressed and ran downstairs. In the sitting room beside the toy cabinet stood her godpapa. Beside him was a handsome young man just her age. His eyes were as blue and kind as those of her own dear nutcracker. Marie knew that she had not been dreaming after all.

Godpapa Drosselmier left the two children alone. Then his nephew knelt before Marie. "Dear Marie Stahlbaum," he said, "by pledging to be my friend despite my ugliness, you have broken Dame Mouserink's curse. Now I beg you to be my friend always and to rule with me over my kingdom."

Marie smiled and said, "Oh, yes!" And when she was grown up, she married young Drosselmier. Then they went to the Marzipan Castle, and today they still rule over the magical Kingdom of Toyland.

THE THREE LITTLE PIGS

Retold by JENNIFER GREENWAY

Illustrated by DEBBIE DIENEMAN

Once upon a time, there were three little pigs who lived in a broken-down cottage with their mother. As they were very poor, the three little pigs decided that it was none too early for them to go into the world and seek their fortunes. So the first little pig packed his favorite belongings, said good-bye to his mother, and set off.

He hadn't gone far before he came to a fine road paved with stones.

"What a beautiful road," said the first little pig. "I believe I will walk down it and see what I can find."

After a while the first little pig came upon a man carrying a big bundle of straw.

"Good morning, sir," said the first little pig. "Please sell me that bundle of straw so that I can make myself a house."

"Certainly," said the man.

So the first little pig gave the man all his money, and the man gave him the bundle of straw.

The first little pig got right to work. He lashed the straw to a coil. Then he wound the coil round and round to build up the walls. Soon the first little pig had made himself a cozy little house of straw, and he was very pleased.

But just as the first little pig was sitting down to his first supper in his new home, along came a big, bad wolf. The wolf had been hunting in the woods all day without finding anything to eat, and he was very hungry. When he saw the little pig's house, he thought, "Now I have found my supper!" The wolf knocked on the little pig's door and cried:

Little pig, little pig!
Let me in!

The first little pig peered out the window. When he saw the big, bad wolf, he said:

No, indeed, I won't let you in!
Not by the hair of my chinny-chin-chin!

That made the wolf cross. So he growled in a very loud voice:

Then I'll huff and I'll puff,
And I'll blow your house down!

But the first little pig still wouldn't let him in. So the big, bad wolf huffed and he puffed until the little house of straw came tumbling down. The first little pig had to run away as fast as he could, or the wolf would have surely eaten him up!

Shortly afterward, the second little pig decided it was time for him to seek his fortune. So he said good-bye to his mother and off he went.

He soon came to a road that was freshly paved with gravel. "What a nice, new road," thought the second little pig. "I believe I will walk down it and see what I can find."

So he turned onto the new gravel road.

Before long, the second little pig came upon a man carrying a big bundle of sticks.

"Good morning, sir," said the second little pig. "Please sell me that bundle of sticks so I can build myself a house."

"Certainly," said the man.

So the second little pig gave the man all his money. Then he took the bundle of sticks and got to work.

The second little pig sawed the sticks neatly. Then he nailed them together. Before long he had made himself a cozy little house of sticks.

But no sooner had the second little pig finished putting on the front door than along came the big, bad wolf.

The wolf knocked loudly at the door and cried:

Little pig, little pig!
Let me in!

When the second little pig peeked out of the window and saw the big, bad wolf, he replied:

No, indeed, I won't let you in!
Not by the hair of my chinny-chin-chin!

That made the wolf cross. So the wolf growled in a very loud voice:

Then I'll huff and I'll puff,
And I'll blow your house down!

The second little pig was frightened, but he still wouldn't let the wolf in.

So the big, bad wolf began to huff and puff.

He huffed and he puffed and he puffed and he huffed.

Before long, the big, bad wolf blew down the second little pig's house of sticks—right down to the ground.

The second little pig had to run away as fast as he could, or the big, bad wolf would have surely eaten him up!

After a while, the third little pig decided it was time for him to go into the world and seek his fortune.

So he packed his belongings and said good-bye to his mother. Then off he went.

After a while he came to a small dirt road. "What a quiet little road," the third little pig said to himself. "I believe I shall go down it and see what I can find."

So the third little pig walked down the dirt road.

Soon he came upon a man carrying a big load of bricks.

"Good morning, sir," said the third little pig. "Please sell me your load of bricks so I can build myself a house."

"Certainly," said the man.

So the third little pig gave the man all his money, and the man gave him the bricks.

The third little pig mixed up some cement, and he carefully laid the bricks one on top of the other. Before long, the little pig had built himself a cozy, sturdy little house of bricks.

No sooner had the third little pig gone inside than along came the big, bad wolf. The wolf knocked on the door as loudly as he could and cried:

Little pig, little pig!
Let me in!

But the third little pig had seen the big, bad wolf coming, and so he replied:

No, indeed, I won't let you in.
Not by the hair of my chinny-chin-chin!

The wolf was very cross when he heard that! So he growled in a big voice:

Then I'll huff and I'll puff
And I'll blow your house down!

Then the wolf huffed and puffed. And he puffed and he huffed. And he huffed and he puffed some more. But no matter how hard he tried, he could not blow down the little house of bricks! So the wolf climbed onto the roof and stuck his head down the chimney.

"I am just poking my nose inside," he said.

"As you like," said the third little pig.

"Now I am just putting my ears inside," said the wolf.

"Fine with me," said the third little pig.

"Now I am just putting my paws inside," said the wolf.

"Very well," said the third little pig.

"Now I am just putting my tail inside," said the wolf. And he fell down the third little pig's chimney!

Suddenly, the wolf gave a terrible howl, for the clever little pig had set a big kettle of water to boil in the fireplace!

The big, bad wolf had to scramble back up the chimney as fast as he could, for otherwise, he surely would have been boiled alive in the third little pig's big kettle.

And so the big, bad wolf ran away, and the third little pig lived happily ever after in his cozy, sturdy little house of bricks!

SLEEPING BEAUTY

Retold by SAMANTHA EASTON

Illustrated by LYNN BYWATERS

Once upon a time there lived a king and queen who longed to have a child. After many years their wish came true, and the queen gave birth to a beautiful baby girl.

The king was beside himself with joy, and he planned a splendid feast in honor of his newborn daughter. He invited all his relatives and all the great lords and ladies of the kingdom.

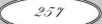

The king also invited the magic fairies who lived in the kingdom. He hoped they would give his child their blessing.

Now there were thirteen fairies in the kingdom, but only twelve received invitations to the feast. Somehow the king forgot to send an invitation to the thirteenth.

The twelve fairies came to the great celebration, and each presented her magical gift to the king's daughter. The first fairy gave the child beauty, the second a kind heart, the third a quick wit, the fourth

charm. And on it went,
until the king's daughter had
received every delightful
talent and trait.

But after the eleventh
fairy had given her gift, the
thirteenth fairy stormed into
the hall. She was furious that
she had not been invited to
the feast. Without a word of
greeting, she turned to the
king and shouted in a harsh
voice, "I, too, have come to
give the princess a gift. On
her fifteenth birthday, your
daughter will prick herself on
a spindle and fall dead!"

And at that the thirteenth fairy turned and strode out of the palace.

The queen began to cry and the king turned pale. But then the twelfth fairy stepped forward.

"I have not given the princess my gift yet," the twelfth fairy said, "and while I cannot undo the curse, I can soften it. Your daughter will not die when she pricks her finger. Instead, she will fall into a deep sleep that will last for one hundred years."

The king, who wished to save his beloved daughter from this fate, immediately ordered all the spinning wheels and spindles in the kingdom to be burned at once.

Years passed and the little princess grew. As the fairies had promised she was beautiful and kind and clever, and each year she grew more charming and lovely. Everyone who knew her loved her and she passed her days happily in the kingdom.

On the day of the princess's fifteenth birthday, her parents' presence was requested by a neighboring king. So they left the princess behind in the castle. "Now you must behave yourself while we are gone," her mother told her.

"Of course," the princess promised.

But the princess had never been without her parents before and she was delighted. "I will be able to wander about the castle as I please," she thought, "and look at everything."

All that day the princess amused herself exploring the castle. She followed every unused corridor she could find and peered into forgotten dusty rooms.

At last, she found herself at the foot of a small winding staircase. She climbed the stairs until she came to an old wooden door with a rusty key in the lock. The princess turned the key and slowly pushed the door open.

Inside, a very, very old woman sat before a spinning wheel. The princess had never seen a spinning wheel and was very curious about it. The old woman was busily spinning thread onto the spindle. The wheel whirred around so merrily that the princess could not help exclaiming, "How wonderful! What is this, Grandmother? What are you doing?"

"Ah," the old woman replied. "This is a spinning wheel and this is a spindle and I am spinning thread."

The princess watched in admiration as the spindle filled with bright thread. "May I please try?" she asked.

Then she reached for the twirling spindle, and in her eagerness she pricked her finger.

"Oh!" she cried, letting go of the spindle. She suddenly felt very sleepy, and for a moment she was sure the old woman was laughing at her.

"Dear me, Grandmother," the princess cried. "I feel so strange! Let me lie down on that bed in the corner." Within moments she had fallen into a deep, deep sleep.

This sleep seemed to creep softly and silently through the castle like a quiet mist. The king and queen, who had just returned, began to yawn. Then slowly closing their eyes, they too slept. The same thing happened to their courtiers and footmen and ladies-in-waiting, until the whole court had fallen asleep where they stood.

The guards at the palace gate let their swords slide from their hands as they slipped into a deep sleep. The palace dogs and cats curled up and closed their eyes. The horses slumbered in their stables. The birds on the rooftop stopped chirping and tucked their heads under their wings. Even the flies stopped buzzing and lay still.

In the kitchen, the cook fell asleep just as she was reaching out to box the scullery boy's ears. He fell asleep, too. So did the kitchen maid, who was sitting at the fire basting some chickens on a spit.

Even the fire in the hearth stopped its crackling and died away. The wind outside stopped blowing. Soon the entire castle was quiet and covered with a blanket of sleep.

Then thick, thorny vines sprang up around the castle. They grew and grew, higher and higher each day, until nothing could be seen of the castle anymore—not its golden gates or its high stone walls or the tops of its golden towers or even the bright flags that flew from them.

Finally the castle was completely covered by a thick screen of thorns.

Across the land people spoke in whispers of the castle hidden behind the thorns. They whispered of the princess who lay inside the palace in a deep enchanted sleep, and they called her the Sleeping Beauty.

Soon princes from far and wide came to the castle. They longed to see Sleeping Beauty with their own

eyes and tried to break through the thick, thorny vines.

And while all these princes were brave and strong, none of them was able to reach the enchanted castle. Whenever they tried to hack through the thicket, the vines clung together so tightly that no sword could cut through them. Many a brave prince became trapped in the thorns and died.

Many years passed. One day, a handsome young prince came riding through the country near the kingdom. He happened to hear an old man telling the story of the enchanted castle hidden behind the thorns. When the old man spoke of Sleeping Beauty, the prince felt a great longing to see her.

"Where is this castle?" he asked the old man. "Please tell me how I might find it!"

The old man begged him not to go there. "I can see that you are brave," he told the prince. "But many a king's son as brave and fair as you has died trying to glimpse the Sleeping Beauty."

Then he told the prince how the great thorny vines closed so tightly around all who tried to pass that they could not escape.

"I am not afraid," the prince replied. "I must see Sleeping Beauty!"

So the old man sighed and told him the way to the castle.

When the prince found the castle, the hundred years were just ending. The day had come when Sleeping Beauty was to awaken.

As the prince approached the thicket, beautiful roses suddenly bloomed on its branches. Then the branches parted to let him pass.

The prince rode through the castle gates, across the sleeping courtyard, and up to the palace. Leaving his horse, he walked through the throne room and past the sleeping king and queen. In every hall and room he entered, not one living thing stirred. The castle was so quiet that the beating of the prince's heart sounded as loud to him as the beating of a drum.

At last, he came to a small spiral staircase. Upon climbing it, he found a small wooden door. He

pushed the door open and gasped. There lay Sleeping Beauty. She lay on the bed as fast asleep as she had been for a hundred years. She was so beautiful that the prince could not help bending over to kiss her.

At his kiss, Sleeping Beauty opened her eyes. The prince smiled at her. She gazed deep into his eyes. It seemed to her that somehow she already knew him, for he was the one she had been waiting for all these years. Then the prince took her hand, and together they went down into the castle.

As they walked, the castle sprang to life again. The horses in the courtyard neighed, the dogs barked, the cats purred, and the birds ruffled their feathers and chirped.

The guards sprang to their feet and picked up their swords. And in the kitchen, the cook boxed the scullery boy's ears. The kitchen maid started turning the chickens on the spit, while the fire crackled to life.

The king and queen opened their eyes and looked around in surprise, as did their courtiers and footmen and ladies-in-waiting. The prince asked Sleeping Beauty to be his wife, and she said yes. Their wedding was celebrated that very day, and a more joyous wedding has never been seen. And ever after that the Sleeping Beauty and her prince lived very happily.

RUMPELSTILTSKIN

By THE BROTHERS GRIMM

Retold by JENNIFER GREENWAY

Illustrated by GARY COOLEY

Once long ago there lived a miller who had a beautiful daughter. One day the king of the land happened to be passing by the mill. To make himself seem important to the king, the miller boasted that his daughter knew how to spin straw into gold.

The king, who liked gold very much, was most impressed.

"I should like to meet this daughter of yours," the king said to the miller. "Bring her to my palace tomorrow morning, and we shall see if what you say is true."

When the miller told his daughter what he had done, she was very upset. But there was nothing she could do. So early the next morning she presented herself at the king's palace.

The king led her into a large room that was completely filled with straw. Then he showed her to a spinning wheel and said, "Now you must get to work. But first, let me tell you this. If you have not spun all the straw into gold by tomorrow morning, you will pay with your life." Then the king left the room and locked the door behind him.

As soon as the king was gone, the miller's

beautiful daughter began to cry, despairing that she had no idea how to spin straw into gold. Just as she was sure there was no hope for her, the door of the room creaked open.

A strange little man came walking in. He looked at her and said, "Tell me, miller's daughter, why are you crying?"

"The king has ordered me to spin this straw into gold," she sobbed. "Unless I do he will have me put to death. And I have no idea how to do it!"

"Oh, that is no problem," replied the strange little man. "What will you give me if I do it for you?"

The miller's daughter stared at him in astonishment. "I . . . I will give you my necklace!" she replied.

"Very well," said the little man and he accepted the necklace. Then he sat down at the spinning wheel and quickly set it whirring. Round and round it turned. Soon the bobbin was full of gold thread. Then the little man put another bobbin on the spinning wheel. Soon that one was full, too. And on he

went all night long until he had spun all the straw into shining gold thread!

The miller's daughter was overjoyed, and she thanked the little man with all her heart. Then, as the sun rose over the horizon, the strange little man vanished.

Soon the king came to see if the miller's daughter had spun the straw into gold. When he saw all the gold thread, he was amazed and delighted. Yet the sight of so much gold only made the king greedier. So he led the miller's daughter to another room.

This room was larger than the first and also filled with straw. "You must spin all this straw into gold by morning," the king told the miller's daughter, "or you will lose your life."

As soon as the king had gone and locked the door behind him, the miller's daughter burst into tears.

Then the door slowly opened, and in walked the same strange little man.

"Good day, miller's daughter," he said. "What will you give me if I spin the straw into gold for you this time?"

"I . . . I will give you my ring!" she replied.

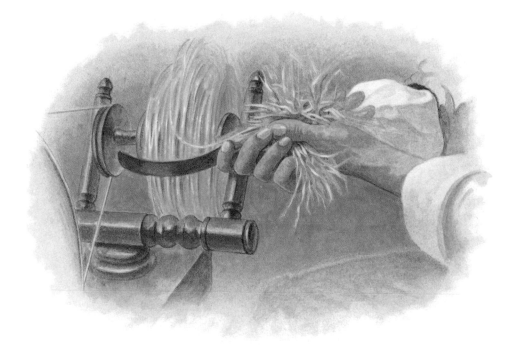

So the strange little man accepted the ring from the young woman's finger. Then he sat down at the spinning wheel and began spinning the straw into gold. And as soon as he was finished he disappeared.

Soon after dawn, the king came to see if the miller's daughter had completed her task. His eyes grew wide at the brilliance of the gold. But it only made him want to have more. So he led the miller's daughter to a third room.

This room was even larger, and it was piled to the ceiling with straw.

"You must spin all this straw into gold before the sun rises tomorrow," the king told the miller's daughter. "If you fail, you will lose your life. But if you succeed I will marry you and make you my wife." The king was thinking to himself that though she was only a miller's daughter, he would never find a richer wife anywhere.

After the king had left the miller's daughter and locked the door behind him, the strange little man once again appeared.

"What will you give me this time for spinning all this straw into gold?" he asked the miller's daughter.

The girl began to sob. "I have nothing left to give you," she answered.

"It is all right," said the little man. "Just promise me this: that when you are queen, you will give me your first child."

The miller's daughter hesitated. Then she gave the strange little man her promise. "Who knows if I shall ever be queen," she thought. "Besides, if I do not agree, then I will surely lose my life tomorrow."

So the little man sat down at the spinning wheel and set it turning. On and on it whirred until all the straw in the room had been spun into shining gold.

The next morning the king came in and saw the immense gold treasure shimmering like the light of a thousand suns. He married the miller's beautiful daughter that very day. She was now a queen with fine robes and a crown on her head.

Within a year, the queen gave birth to a beautiful baby boy. She was overjoyed to have a child of her own. In her happiness, she forgot her promise to the strange little man.

One day, as the queen was playing with her baby son, the little man visited her.

"I have come to claim what you promised me," he said, stretching out his arms toward the child.

The queen was horrified. "Please do not take my little son," she pleaded. "I will give you anything— anything you wish. Only leave me my son!"

Then she offered the strange little man all the wealth and riches in the kingdom, if he would only spare her child.

At first, the little man refused. But the queen began to weep so sorrowfully that he took pity on her. "Very well," he said. "I will give you three days to guess my name. If you do so in that time, you may keep your little son. But if you fail, the child must be mine." And with that the strange little man vanished.

The queen stayed awake all night. She thought of every name she had ever heard. Then she took her candle and went to the palace library and searched through all the books for strange and unusual names.

The next morning when the little man appeared, the queen began asking him, "Is your name Peter? Is your name John? Is your name Charlemagne?"

Each time the little man replied, "Oh, no! That is not my name!"

Then the queen recited all the names she knew one after the other. But to each one the little man replied,

"Oh, no! That is not my name!" Finally, she could think of no more names and the little man went away.

The queen summoned to her all the learned men of the king-dom and asked them to tell her all the strange and unusual names they had ever heard. She sent out her servants far and wide to collect as many odd names as they could.

When the little man came the next day, she asked him, "Is your name Big-Boots? Is your name Turtle-Beak? Can your name be Mutton-Chop or Crooked-Knees?"

But to each name the little man replied as before, "Oh, no! That is not my name!"

The queen did not know what to do.

On the third day, one of the queen's servants came to her and told a curious story.

"I searched far and wide, but I could not find a single new name," the man began. "Then on my way back through the mountains I came upon a tiny cottage. A fire was blazing in front of it, and a little man was dancing around the fire on one foot. As he danced, he sang this song:

I'll rest tomorrow and bake today
Then I'll take the queen's son away.
For no one will ever guess who I am
And that Rumpelstiltskin is my name!

The queen clapped her hands for joy.

When the little man came the next morning, she asked him, "Is your name Henry?"

"No!" he replied.

"Is your name Roland?"

"No!"

"Then can your name be . . . Rumpelstiltskin?"

The little man's mouth fell open. "Who told you that? Who told you that?" he shrieked.

And he became so cross, he tugged at his little beard and stamped his foot. He stamped so hard that the ground cracked open beneath him and swallowed him up! And that was the last anyone ever saw of Rumpelstiltskin!

Mother Goose's Nursery Rhymes

Illustrated by ROBYN OFFICER

*H*ERE WE GO *round the mulberry bush,*
The mulberry bush, the mulberry bush.
Here we go round the mulberry bush,
On a cold and frosty morning.

*H*EY Diddle, Diddle,

The cat and the fiddle,

The cow jumped over the moon;

The little dog laughed

To see such sport

And the dish ran away with the spoon.

*I*TSY bitsy spider, climbed up the water spout,
Down came the rain and washed poor spider out.
Out came the sun and dried up all the rain;
And the itsy bitsy spider, climbed up the spout again.

*R*ING around the roses,
A pocket full of posies;
Ashes, ashes!
We all fall down.

*T*HREE blind mice, see how they run!
They all ran after the farmer's wife,
Who cut off their tails with a carving knife.
Did you ever see such a sight in your life,
As three blind mice?

*T*HERE *was an old woman who lived in a shoe,*
She had so many children she didn't know what to do;
She gave them some broth without any bread;
She whipped them all soundly and put them to bed.

*J*ACK *and Jill went up the hill*
To fetch a pail of water;
Jack fell down and broke his crown,
And Jill came tumbling after.

The Night Before Christmas

By CLEMENT C. MOORE

Illustrated by LYNN FERRIS

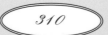

'Twas the night before Christmas, when all through the house
Not a creature was stirring, not even a mouse.

The stockings were hung by the chimney with care,
In hopes that St. Nicholas soon would be there.
The children were nestled all snug in their beds,
While visions of sugarplums danced in their heads;

And Mama in her kerchief, and I in my cap,
Had just settled our brains for a long winter's nap,
When out on the lawn there arose such a clatter,
I sprang from my bed to see what was the matter.
Away to the window I flew like a flash,
Tore open the shutters and threw up the sash.
The moon on the breast of the new-fallen snow
Gave a luster of midday to objects below;

When what to my wondering eyes should appear
But a miniature sleigh and eight tiny reindeer,
With a little old driver, so lively and quick,
I knew in a moment it must be St. Nick!

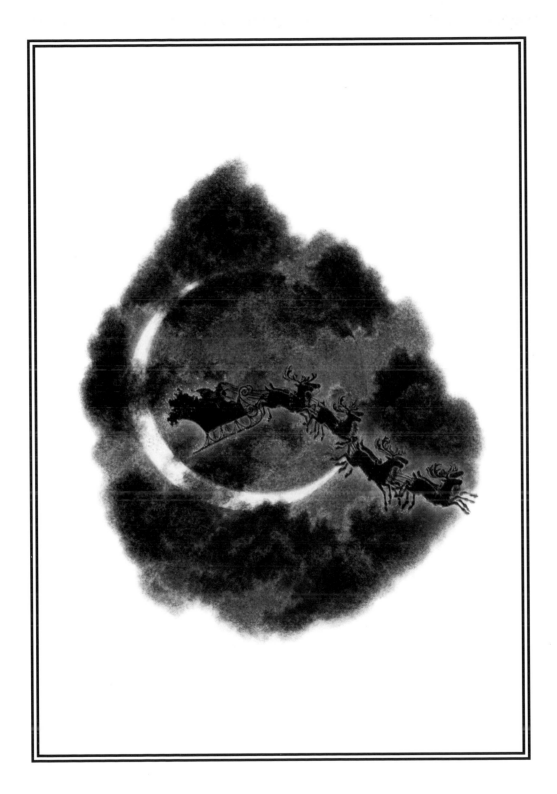

More rapid than eagles his coursers they came,
And he whistled and shouted and called them by name:
"Now, Dasher! Now, Dancer! Now, Prancer and Vixen!
On, Comet! On, Cupid! On, Donder and Blitzen!
To the top of the porch! To the top of the wall!
Now dash away! Dash away! Dash away, all!"

As dry leaves that before the wild hurricane fly,

When they meet with an obstacle, mount to the sky,

So up to the housetop the coursers they flew,

With a sleigh full of toys—and St. Nicholas too.

And then, in a twinkling, I heard on the roof

The prancing and pawing of each little hoof.

As I drew in my head and was turning around,

Down the chimney St. Nicholas came with a bound.

He was dressed all in fur, from his head to his foot,
And his clothes were all tarnished with ashes and soot;
A bundle of toys he had flung on his back,
And he looked like a peddler just opening his pack.
His eyes, how they twinkled! His dimples, how merry!
His cheeks were like roses, his nose like a cherry!
His droll little mouth was drawn up like a bow,
And the beard on his chin was as white as the snow.
The stump of a pipe he held tight in his teeth,
And the smoke, it encircled his head like a wreath.

He had a broad face and a little round belly
That shook, when he laughed, like a bowl full of jelly.
He was chubby and plump, a right jolly old elf,
And I laughed when I saw him, in spite of myself.
A wink of his eye and a twist of his head
Soon gave me to know I had nothing to dread.

He spoke not a word, but went straight to his work,
And filled all the stockings, then turned with a jerk,
And laying a finger aside of his nose,
And giving a nod, up the chimney he rose.

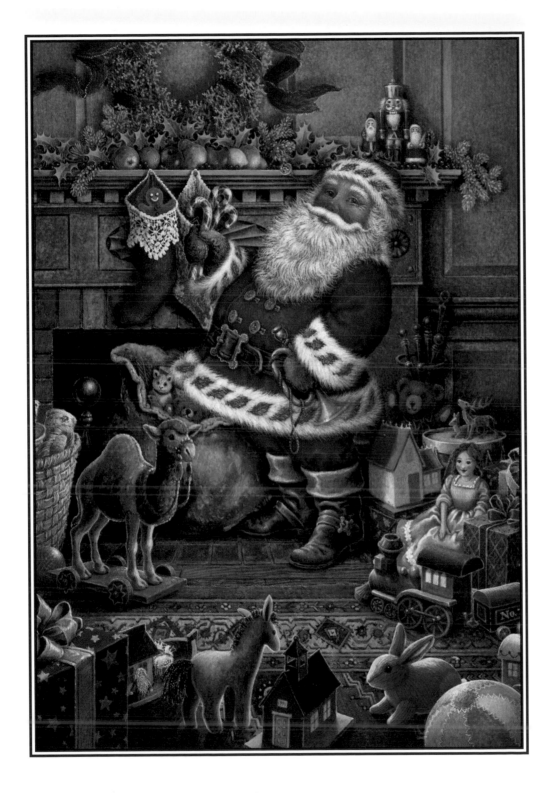

He sprang to his sleigh, to his team gave a whistle,
And away they all flew like the down of a thistle.
But I heard him exclaim, ere he drove out of sight,
"Happy Christmas to all, and to all a good night!"

GOLDILOCKS
and the
THREE BEARS

Retold by JENNIFER GREENWAY

Illustrated by ELIZABETH MILES

Once upon a time there were three bears who lived in a cottage in the woods. There was a great big Papa Bear, a medium-sized Mama Bear, and a little tiny Baby Bear.

One morning the three bears cooked themselves some porridge for breakfast. Then, as the porridge was much too hot to eat, they went for a walk in the woods while it cooled.

No sooner had they gone, than along came a little girl named Goldilocks.

Goldilocks had been playing in the woods and had gotten lost. When she saw the three bears' cottage, her eyes lit up.

"What a pretty little cottage," she said to herself. "I wonder who lives there?"

So Goldilocks went up to the cottage and knocked on the door. She waited quite a long time, but there was no answer.

Goldilocks walked around to the side of the cottage. She stood on her tiptoes, pressed her face to the window, and peered in. She could not see anyone. She stood still and listened carefully, but she could hear no one. So she hurried back to the front door, turned the knob, and walked in!

The first thing Goldilocks saw was a table set with three bowls of porridge. There was a great big bowl for Papa Bear, a medium-sized bowl for Mama Bear, and a little tiny bowl for Baby Bear.

Now Goldilocks was very fond of porridge, and her walk had made her hungry. So she took a taste of the porridge in the great big bowl.

But that porridge was much too hot!

"Ouch!" cried Goldilocks, dropping the spoon.

Next Goldilocks took a taste of the porridge in the medium-sized bowl.

But that porridge was much too cold!

"How nasty," said Goldilocks, making a horrible face. Then she took a taste of the porridge in the little tiny bowl.

That porridge was just right!

"Mmmm," said Goldilocks, with a smile. "This porridge is very tasty!" Then she took another spoonful and another and another. And before Goldilocks knew what she was doing, she had eaten Baby Bear's porridge all up!

Then Goldilocks saw three chairs set before the fireplace. There was a great big chair that belonged to Papa Bear, a medium-sized chair that belonged to Mama Bear, and a little tiny chair that belonged to Baby Bear.

Goldilocks climbed into Papa Bear's great big chair.

"Ouch," she cried, jumping down at once. "That chair is much too hard!"

Next Goldilocks climbed into Mama Bear's medium-sized chair.

"Oh," she cried, as she sank down into the cushions. "This chair is much too soft!"

Then Goldilocks climbed into Baby Bear's little tiny chair.

"Ah," she said, and she smiled and leaned back. "This chair is just right!"

But just as Goldilocks was beginning to feel comfortable, down she tumbled with a crash!

"Oh dear," cried Goldilocks, for Baby Bear's little tiny chair was broken into a thousand pieces!

Next Goldilocks climbed the stairs to the three bears' bedroom. There she saw three beds all in a row. There was a great big bed for Papa Bear, a medium-sized bed for Mama Bear, and a little tiny bed for Baby Bear.

First, Goldilocks climbed into Papa Bear's great big bed and pulled down the covers.

But she jumped down right away.

"Oh no," Goldilocks said. "That bed is much too hard!"

Then she climbed into Mama Bear's medium-sized bed. "Oh dear," said Goldilocks, wrinkling her nose. "This bed is much too soft!"

Then Goldilocks went to Baby Bear's little tiny bed, pulled down the covers, and climbed in.

That bed was just right!

Goldilocks closed her eyes, and soon she was fast asleep.

Then the three bears returned from their walk. They were very hungry and were looking forward to a breakfast of delicious porridge.

As soon as they came inside, the three bears washed their hands and sat down at the table.

Papa Bear stared down at his great big bowl. Then he said in his great big voice, "Someone has been eating my porridge!"

Mama Bear looked down at her bowl. "Oh dear," she said in her medium-sized voice, "someone has been eating my porridge!"

Then Baby Bear looked down at his little tiny bowl. "Someone has been eating my porridge," he cried in his little tiny voice, "and they've eaten it all up!"

Then the three bears walked to their three chairs that were set before the fireplace.

Just as Papa Bear was about to sit down in his great big chair, he growled in his great big voice, "Someone has been sitting in my chair!"

And just as Mama Bear was about to sit down in her medium-sized chair, she cried out in her medium-sized voice, "Someone has been sitting in my chair!"

Baby Bear looked down at his little tiny chair. "Someone has been sitting in my chair," he cried in his little tiny voice, "and they've broken it into a thousand pieces!"

Next the three bears went upstairs to the bedroom.

Papa Bear looked at his great big bed and saw that the covers had been pulled down. Then he frowned and growled in his great big voice, "Someone has been sleeping in my bed!"

Then Mama Bear looked at her medium-sized bed and saw that the pillows had been scattered about.

"And someone has been sleeping in my bed," Mama Bear cried in her medium-sized voice.

Baby Bear looked at his little tiny bed. "And someone has been sleeping in my bed!" he cried in his little tiny voice, "AND HERE SHE IS!"

When Goldilocks heard Baby Bear's little tiny voice, she awoke with a start. She looked up and saw the three bears standing around her.

Goldilocks was so frightened that she leaped out of bed, raced down the stairs, and dashed out the door of the three bears' cottage. And she didn't stop running until she was all the way home.

Then the three bears fixed themselves another breakfast of hot porridge. And they never saw Goldilocks again!

Snow White

By THE BROTHERS GRIMM

Retold by JENNIFER GREENWAY

Illustrated by ERIN AUGENSTINE

*O*ne snowy winter day, a queen sat at the window sewing on a frame made of ebony. She pricked her finger with the needle, and three drops of blood fell in the snow on the windowsill.

The red blood looked so beautiful against the white snow that the queen exclaimed, "I wish I had a daughter as white as snow, red as blood, and black as ebony."

A short time later the queen gave birth to a
daughter whose skin was as white as snow, whose
cheeks were as red as blood, and whose hair was black
as ebony. She named her child Snow White and not
long after, the queen died.

Snow White grew up to be the most beautiful girl
in the world. She was so good and kind that everyone
who met her could not help but love her. Even the
birds in the trees and the animals of the woods
adored her.

When Snow White was still a child, her father
took a second wife. She was a very beautiful woman,
but proud and spiteful. She could not bear the
thought that anyone else might be as beautiful as she.

Now this queen had a magic mirror and whenever she looked into it, she would say:

Mirror, mirror, on the wall,
Who's the fairest of them all?

And the mirror would reply:

You are the fairest of them all.

Each year, however, Snow White grew more beautiful. One day, when the queen looked into her mirror and asked it who was the fairest of them all, the mirror replied:

You are very fair, 'tis true.
But Snow White is more fair than you!

When the queen heard that she turned green with envy.

The queen called her huntsman before her. "You are to take Snow White into the forest," she said. "Kill her there, for I do not wish to set eyes on her again. And bring me the girl's heart in this box as proof that you have done as I have ordered."

The huntsman then led Snow White deep into the forest. But as he was drawing his hunting knife to kill her, Snow White cried, "Please spare my life! Let me run away into the forest and I will never come home again!"

Snow White was so young that the huntsman took pity on her. He said to her, "Run into the woods, dear child!" Then he killed a deer and took its heart to the wicked queen as proof that Snow White was dead.

After he had gone, Snow White was alone in the forest. She was so frightened by the shapes of the trees and the rustling of the leaves that she began to run. Wild beasts sprang at her, but they did her no harm.

On she ran, over rocks and through brambles, until it began to grow dark. Snow White was so tired, she thought she could not take another step. Then up ahead she saw a tiny cottage.

Snow White went inside. Everything in the cottage was very clean and tidy—and also very small. There was a little table covered with a white cloth and set with seven little plates, each with a spoon and a knife and a cup. And against the wall, all in a row, were seven little beds.

Snow White was very hungry and thirsty. So she ate a bit of bread from each plate and drank a drop of water from each cup, for she did not want to take everything from any single one.

Then, as she was very tired, she lay down on one of the beds. Soon she was fast asleep.

A short while later, the owners of the cottage came home. They were seven dwarfs who spent their days mining in the mountains. As soon as they lit their candles the dwarfs saw that someone had been there while they were out.

"Who has been eating from my plate?" said the first.

"Who has been drinking from my cup?" cried the second.

And on it went, until the seventh dwarf caught sight of Snow White fast asleep in his bed. He called the others over, and they all stood and stared in wonder at the sleeping child.

"How beautiful she is!" they whispered, and they decided to let her go on sleeping.

The next morning, Snow White was frightened when she woke up and saw the seven dwarfs. But they smiled kindly at her and asked her her name.

"Snow White," she replied. Then she told them how her wicked stepmother had ordered the huntsman to kill her and how he had spared her her life.

"Why don't you stay here with us?" the dwarfs said. "You can cook and keep house for us, and we will take good care of you."

Snow White agreed, and so she kept the cottage for them and always had supper ready when they came home from working in the mountains.

As Snow White was alone all day, the dwarfs warned her to be careful.

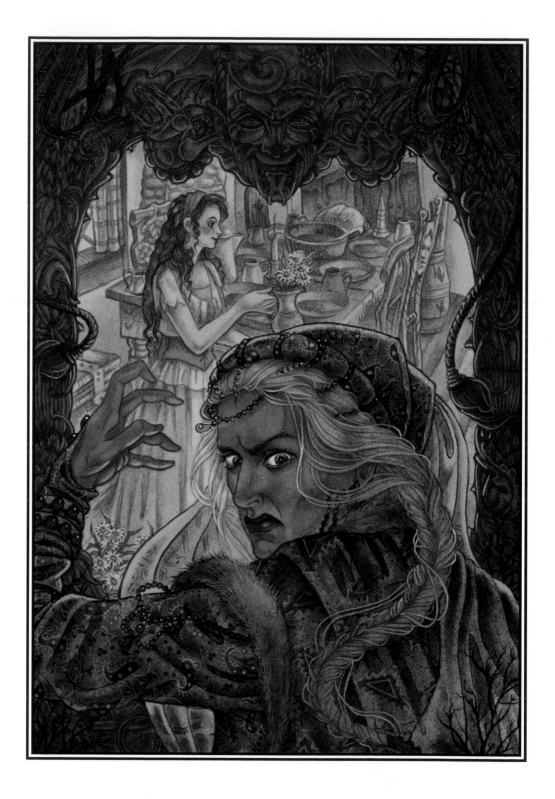

"Do not let anyone in," they said, "for your wicked stepmother will surely discover where you are and come looking for you."

At that very moment the wicked queen looked into her magic mirror and asked:

Mirror, mirror, on the wall,
Who's the fairest one of all?

And the mirror replied:

You are very fair, 'tis true.
But in a cottage far away,
Where the seven dwarfs do stay,
Snow White is fairer still than you!

The wicked queen shook with rage. Snow White lived. Her magic mirror never lied. All day she schemed, until at last she settled on a plan to get rid of Snow White.

First the wicked queen made a poisoned apple. Half of it was snow-white and the other half was rosy red, and it looked delicious.

When the apple was ready, the queen disguised herself as a poor farm woman. Then she traveled to the seven dwarfs' cottage.

When the queen knocked on the door, Snow White came to the window.

"I cannot let anyone in," Snow White called out.

"But I only wish to sell you some of my apples," replied the farm woman. "Here, try one!" And she held out the poisoned apple.

But Snow White said, "No. I dare not!"

"Are you afraid I might poison you?" laughed the farm woman. "Look, I will cut the apple in two. You take the rosy red half, and I'll take the white." But Snow White did not know that the red half was poisoned.

"Very well," Snow White said, for the apple looked so delicious, she could not help herself. Eagerly, she bit into it. No sooner had she done so, than she fell down dead.

When the seven dwarfs came home that night they found Snow White lying pale and still on the ground. They called her name and tried to shake her awake, but it was no use. Snow White was truly dead.

At the palace, the wicked queen gazed into her magic mirror and asked who was the fairest of them all. The mirror replied:

You are the fairest of them all.

Finally, the wicked queen was satisfied.

The seven dwarfs wept over Snow White for three days. Then, it was time to bury her. But she looked as if she were still alive, and they could not bear to put her in the cold ground. So they made her a glass coffin and wrote her name on it in gold letters. Then they set it in the forest.

For a long time, Snow White lay in the glass coffin. Yet her beauty did not fade. One day a prince rode into the forest and saw the coffin. Snow White looked so lovely that he fell in love with her.

The prince begged the dwarfs to let him have Snow White's coffin. At last, they took pity on him and agreed.

The prince ordered his servants to carry Snow White in her glass coffin to his palace. But on the way, one of them tripped. The coffin fell, and the piece of poisoned apple flew from Snow White's throat.

Snow White opened her eyes. "Where am I?" she cried, looking up at the prince.

"You are with me," he replied, "and I wish you to marry me and stay with me forever."

The prince looked so kind and sincere that Snow White said, "Yes." And their wedding was celebrated with great joy. The seven dwarfs all came and danced and cheered.

As for the wicked queen, she was so angry that she ran into the forest and was never seen again. And with no one to wish them harm, Snow White and the prince lived happily ever after.

CINDERELLA

Retold by SAMANTHA EASTON

Illustrated by LYNN BYWATERS

Once upon a time there lived a rich but meek man whose wife had died. After a time, he married again. His second wife was very proud and ill-tempered, and she had two daughters who were just like her.

Now, this man had a daughter from his first marriage. She was very good and beautiful, which made her stepmother and stepsisters jealous.

It wasn't long before the stepmother and her daughters began to treat the poor girl very badly. They made her do the cooking and cleaning, and gave her only an old gray smock to wear. Instead of sleeping in a bed, she had to sleep on the hearth among the cinders. And that was how she came to be called Cinderella.

One day, Cinderella's stepsisters received invitations to a ball that the king was giving for his son. All the young ladies of the kingdom were invited, for the prince wished to choose one of them as his bride.

Cinderella's stepsisters were overjoyed. From that moment on, they could talk of nothing except what they would wear to the ball.

"I shall wear my gold embroidered gown," said the elder. "The prince will surely notice me in that!"

"And I shall wear my red velvet gown," said the younger. "Mother has always told me I look best in red!"

And on and on they talked and planned. They were each determined to be the most beautiful lady at the ball.

At last, the day arrived.

All day Cinderella's stepsisters shouted orders at her. "Cinderella, iron my silk petticoat!" said one. "Curl my hair!" said the other. "Tie this ribbon!" said the first. "Polish my shoes!" said the other. Cinderella didn't complain but did their every bidding.

At last her stepsisters were dressed and ready. As she saw them to the door, Cinderella could not help but sigh, "How I wish I were going to the ball."

Her stepsisters stared at her. "You?" mocked the elder. "What an idea. How could you go to the ball?"

"Besides, whatever would you wear?" said the younger. "Your tattered gray dress with your patched apron?"

Then they both burst into laughter and stepped into their coach.

After her stepsisters had gone, Cinderella sat by the hearth and cried.

Then a voice beside her asked, "Cinderella, why are you crying?"

Cinderella looked up. There stood an old woman wearing a white dress covered with silver stars. In her hand she held a sparkling wand. "I am crying because . . ." she stammered.

"Because you would like to go to the ball," the old woman finished for her. "And so you shall. I am your fairy godmother and I have come here tonight to make all your wishes come true."

Before Cinderella could say another word, her fairy godmother led her into the pumpkin patch in the garden. "First, we must choose a large, round pumpkin," she said. "That one looks about right!"

As Cinderella watched in amazement, her fairy godmother waved her magic wand over the pumpkin and it was transformed into a gold coach!

"Now," said Cinderella's fairy godmother, "let us find the mousetrap and see if there are any mice."

Inside the trap were six gray mice. The fairy godmother waved her magic wand again, and in the twinkling of an eye, they were turned into six fine dappled horses.

"Now, let's look in the rattrap," said the fairy godmother. Inside there was a fat white rat. The fairy godmother touched it with her wand, and instead there stood a jolly coachman with wonderful long whiskers.

"Now, go to the lily pond," Cinderella's fairy god-mother told her. "If you find six green frogs sitting on a log, bring them to me."

And Cinderella did so. With a wave of her magic wand, her fairy godmother turned the frogs into six merry footmen, all dressed in handsome suits of green.

Cinderella was overjoyed. But then she looked down at her old gray smock and her face fell.

"Don't worry!" her fairy godmother said kindly. "I have thought of that, too."

She waved her magic wand once more, and the tattered gray smock became the most beautiful gown Cinderella had ever seen. The dress was made of silver and gold, and was studded with precious gems. Then her fairy godmother brought from her pocket a pair of sparkling glass slippers.

"Now, you are ready to go to the ball," she said with a smile. "But be warned! You must return before the clock strikes twelve. At that hour my magic will fade. Your gold coach will turn back into a pumpkin. Your horses will be mice, your coachman, a rat, and your footmen, only frogs. And your beautiful gown will once again be a tattered gray smock."

Cinderella gave her promise. Then she thanked her fairy godmother and set off happily to the king's palace.

When Cinderella entered the king's great ball-room, she looked so lovely that everyone stopped talking and eating to look at her.

"Who can she be?" they whispered. Her stepsisters, who did not recognize her, said that Cinderella must be a princess from a faraway land. "Who else would be wearing such a splendid gown?" they murmured.

The prince had never seen such a beautiful lady. Immediately, he introduced himself to her and asked her to dance.

Cinderella smiled and nodded. She danced so gracefully that everyone stopped dancing and watched her in admiration.

All night long the prince danced with Cinderella, and Cinderella only. She had never been so happy. She felt as if she were in a beautiful dream.

Cinderella was enjoying herself so much that she did not notice the time passing. Suddenly, the clock began to strike twelve.

"Good-bye!" she called to the startled prince as she dashed from the ballroom. The prince ran after her, but Cinderella was too quick for him.

In her haste, she lost one of her sparkling glass slippers on the palace steps. But there was no time to stop for anything. Just as she reached the gate, the last stroke of midnight rang out. Her beautiful gown turned back into her old gray smock, and her gold coach became a pumpkin. She watched as the mice and the frogs and the rat scurried off. And then she slowly walked home.

The next morning, the prince found Cinderella's glass slipper on the palace steps. It was the most delicate slipper he had ever seen. He carefully picked it up and carried it to his father. "I will marry only the woman whose foot this slipper fits, and no other," he told the king.

At once the king sent his servants throughout the kingdom to try the glass slipper on each lady.

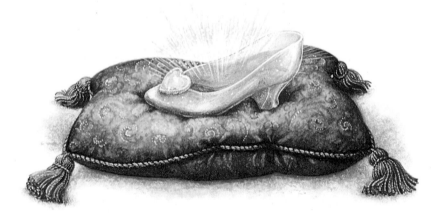

All sorts of young ladies—tall and short, plump and thin, rich and poor—tried on the beautiful glass slipper. But not one of them could get it to fit.

At last, the king's servants came to Cinderella's house. Her two stepsisters were eager to try on the slipper, since they both considered their feet to be small and dainty.

First the elder stepsister tried to get the slipper on, but it would not even go over her toes. She pushed and pulled, but it was no use. Then the younger stepsister tried it on. She tugged and winced, but she could not get the slipper on over her heel.

Then Cinderella said, "May I try, too?"

Her stepsisters rolled their eyes and said, "The slipper will never fit you!"

But the king's servant said that it was only right that she be allowed to try. So Cinderella stretched out her foot.

The stepsisters were surprised. The glass slipper fit Cinderella's foot so perfectly it might just as well have been made for her!

To their further amazement, Cinderella reached into her pocket and brought out the matching glass slipper.

At that moment, Cinderella's fairy godmother appeared, but only Cinderella could see her. With a wave of her magic wand, she turned Cinderella's rags into a gown even more beautiful than the one she had worn to the ball.

Her stepsisters then recognized Cinderella as the lovely princess from the ball. They knelt before her and apologized for treating her so badly. Then Cinderella, who was as kind as she was beautiful, said, "It's all right, sisters. I forgive you both."

The king's servants took Cinderella to the palace to see the prince. He was overjoyed to see her again, and asked her to become his dear wife.

Cinderella and her prince were married that very day. Everyone in the kingdom was invited, even Cinderella's stepmother and stepsisters. It was the most splendid and joyful wedding anyone had ever seen, and Cinderella and her prince lived happily ever after.

THE THREE BILLY
GOATS GRUFF

Retold by JENNIFER GREENWAY

Illustrated by LORETTA LUSTIG

Once upon a time there were three billy goats. The name of these three goats was Gruff, so they were known as the Three Billy Goats Gruff.

The Three Billy Goats Gruff lived in a rocky field at the bottom of a grassy hill. The grass in this field was brown and tough, and the Three Billy Goats Gruff were always hungry.

The Three Billy Goats Gruff wished they could go up the hill to where the grass was green and tender. "If we could only do that," they said, "then we would all become fat and be very happy."

However, to get up the hill, the Three Billy Goats Gruff had to cross a bridge that went over a rushing stream. Under this bridge, there lived a big ugly troll who liked nothing better than to eat billy goats and anything else that crossed his path.

So the Three Billy Goats Gruff stayed where they were. But every day they looked up at the hillside and sighed, for they so longed to go there and enjoy the tender grass.

One day, the youngest Billy Goat Gruff turned to his brothers and said, "I can't bear trying to chew this tough brown grass anymore. I am going to go up the hillside to where the grass is green and sweet!"

"But what about the troll?" exclaimed the other two. "He will surely eat you up!"

"Perhaps he will," the youngest Billy Goat Gruff replied, "But if I stay in this field, I will surely starve anyway! I am going to cross that bridge."

"But you are the smallest of us all!" said the other Billy Goats Gruff. "The troll will be able to eat you with no trouble!"

"We shall see about that," said the youngest Billy Goat Gruff.

So off the youngest Billy Goat Gruff went. When he reached the bridge where the troll lived he started across it as fast as he could. *Tip-tap*, *tip-tap*, *tip-tap* went his tiny little hooves.

The big ugly troll heard something overhead, and just as the youngest Billy Goat Gruff reached the center of the bridge, the troll called out in his big voice:

"Who's that crossing my bridge?"

"It's only me," replied the youngest Billy Goat Gruff in his tiny little voice.

"Is that so?" roared the troll. "Well, I am going to eat you up!"

The youngest Billy Goat Gruff was very frightened, but he replied bravely, "Oh, please don't do that. I am so small and thin, I would hardly be enough for a snack for such a big creature as you."

"You'll do fine," the troll said.

"No," cried the youngest Billy Goat Gruff. "Wait until my brother, the second Billy Goat Gruff, comes along. He is much bigger and fatter than I. He will make you a much better supper!"

The troll was quite hungry, so he agreed to wait. The youngest Billy Goat Gruff continued on his

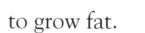

way—*tip-tap, tip-tap, tip-tap*—up the hillside to where the grass grew green and thick. There, the youngest Billy Goat Gruff ate to his heart's content, and he began to grow fat.

After a while, the second Billy Goat Gruff decided he would try his luck. So off he went toward the bridge where the troll lived. When he reached the bridge he started across it as fast as he could. *Trip-trap, trip-trap, trip-trap* went his middle-sized hooves. The troll heard him and cried in his big voice, "Who's that crossing my bridge?"

"It's only me," replied the second Billy Goat Gruff in his middle-sized voice.

"Is that so?" said the troll. "Well, I am going to eat you up!"

The second Billy Goat Gruff was very frightened, but he replied bravely, "Oh, no! Don't do that. I'm not nearly big and fat enough to satisfy such a big fellow like you. Wait until my brother, the third Billy Goat Gruff, comes along. He's much bigger than I, and I'm sure that he will fill you up!"

The troll, who was very hungry by now, agreed to wait once more.

So the second Billy Goat Gruff continued across the bridge—*trip-trap, trip-trap, trip-trap*—and soon he joined his younger brother on the hillside where the grass grew green and sweet.

The second Billy Goat Gruff ate and ate, and before long he was even fatter than his brother.

Now the third Billy Goat Gruff found himself all alone in the dry brown field. He decided to try his luck, too.

So off went the third Billy Goat Gruff toward the bridge where the troll lived.

When the third Billy Goat Gruff reached the bridge, he started across it as fast as he could. *TRAMP, TRAMP, TRAMP* went his big hooves. The big ugly troll heard him, and he cried out in his great big voice, "Who's that crossing my bridge?"

Then the troll poked his head up over the bridge to take a look. When the third Billy Goat Gruff saw him, he thought, "Why, that troll's not so big!" And he replied in his biggest voice, "It's only ME!"

"Is that so?" roared the troll. "Well, I'm going to eat you!"

"Let's see you try it," replied the third Billy Goat Gruff. And then he shouted:

I've got two big sharp horns
that will make you sore!
And two big pronged hooves
that will break your bones!
And lots of big sharp teeth
that will bite you all over!

Now, the troll was so hungry by this time that when he heard what the third Billy Goat said, he got mad! He jumped up onto the bridge and ran straight toward the third Billy Goat Gruff, shouting, "I'm going to eat you up right now!"

So the third Billy Goat Gruff butted the ugly troll with his big sharp horns. Then he kicked the troll with his big pronged hooves. Then he bit him all over with his big sharp teeth.

At last, the troll begged him to stop. "I promise I won't eat you!" he said. "Please, let me go!"

But the third Billy Goat Gruff kept on butting and kicking and biting him until, at last, the big ugly troll jumped off the bridge and was swept away by the rushing stream.

Then the third Billy Goat Gruff continued on his way—*TRAMP, TRAMP, TRAMP*—and soon he reached the hillside where the grass grew thick and green.

There he joined his brothers, and he ate and ate the tender grass and became very, very fat, which made him very, very happy.

So the three Billy Goats Gruff lived on the green hillside, and they all grew fatter and fatter. And for all I know they still live there today.

As for the big ugly troll, no one ever saw or heard of him again!

The text of this book was set in Goudy and the
display in Swanson by Harry Chester, Inc.,
New York City.

Book design by Judith Stagnitto Abbate